70-991
I.

The Serpent's Tooth Mystery

Frank and Joe moved slowly along the roof. Suddenly Frank stopped as their flashlight illuminated some boxes. "Look at these."

"They're like the case the tiger snake came in!" Joe exclaimed. But he noticed something else—an unusual shadow making an S-shaped line in the loose gravel. A chill crawled up his spine.

It was a track, left not by a foot, but by a very large snake. As the brothers inspected the trail, they came to another box.

"I wonder why the thief left this one behind?" Joe mused, reaching out to turn the case. As his fingers touched the edge, Frank slapped Joe's arm away.

At that instant, a hideous angry hiss issued from inside.

The case wasn't empty—and its deadly occupant didn't sound happy!

The Hardy Boys Mystery Stories

Available from MINSTREL Books

93

The

HARDY BOYS®

THE SERPENT'S TOOTH MYSTERY

FRANKLIN W. DIXON

A MINSTREL® BOOK

PUBLISHED BY POCKET BOOKS

New York   London   Toronto   Sydney   Tokyo

This novel is a work of fiction. Names, characters, places and incidents are either the product of the author's imagination or are used fictitiously. Any resemblance to actual events or locales or persons, living or dead, is entirely coincidental.

A MINSTREL PAPERBACK *ORIGINAL*

A Minstrel Book published by
POCKET BOOKS, a division of Simon & Schuster Inc.
1230 Avenue of the Americas, New York, NY 10020

ISBN: 0-671-66310-0

First Minstrel Books printing December 1988

10 9 8 7 6 5 4 3 2

THE HARDY BOYS MYSTERY STORIES is a trademark of Simon & Schuster Inc.

THE HARDY BOYS, A MINSTREL BOOK and colophon are registered trademarks of Simon & Schuster Inc.

Printed in the U.S.A.

Contents

1 The Cohen Connection

"Now where do we go?" Frank Hardy squinted in the early-morning sunlight as he drove along. He ran a hand through his brown hair in confusion, then glanced at his friend in the backseat.

"Take the next left," Phil Cohen told him.

Frank maneuvered the blue van down a tree-lined drive to stop in front of a large steel gate. He stepped out to move it open, then glanced back at his friend. "It's locked."

"Locked?" echoed a muffled voice from the passenger seat. A pair of blue eyes heavy with sleep peeked over the seat back to glare at Phil.

"You drag me out of bed on a Monday morning to sit in front of a locked gate at the zoo?" Joe Hardy, Frank's younger brother, sighed. "Phil, you live dangerously! We detectives need our rest."

Phil inspected Joe's athletic six-foot frame, then shook his head sadly. "Hey, Joe. You *look* like you need it. Go back to sleep."

1

Frank laughed. "You should know better than to take Professor Phil on in a battle of wits. At this hour you're low on ammo."

The word *professor* fit Phil Cohen perfectly. He was Bayport High's resident high-tech genius, knowing everything there was to know about computers and all kinds of electronic gadgets.

"I may not be a tower of intellect," Joe growled, "but at least I know better than to visit the zoo a whole hour before it opens!"

Frank gestured to the gate, a work entrance to Bayport's Zoological Gardens. "Joe has a point, Phil. You make us get up at an unreal hour, babbling about a secret project, and you still haven't told us anything about it."

"Even the animals aren't up yet," Joe added.

Phil chuckled as he stepped out of the van. "When you see the animal we've come for, you may wish it would stay asleep."

"More riddles!" Joe said. "This is it! Grab him, Frank—we'll torture him till he talks!"

"It's no mystery, Joe," said Phil, laughing. "Just a secret addition to the zoo. I thought you guys would like a break from detective work."

"No way!" Frank and Joe said in unison. The Hardys had solved a lot of mysteries with their sharp detective work. Sometimes they even helped their detective father, Fenton Hardy, with cases.

"Okay, I'll talk," Phil said. "You know I've been working for several weeks with Dr. Harrod Michaels, who's a world-famous herpetologist."

"A what?" exclaimed Joe.

"Snake expert," answered Phil. "Dr. Michaels studies venomous animals and their venoms. He's especially interested in the cobra family. My job has been to build a specially designed, climate-controlled display case for a new arrival."

"New arrival?" Frank said.

"It's an Australian tiger snake." Phil's voice was sober. "This may be the most deadly reptile on earth. The only other specimen in the United States is in California. Our snake will need time to settle down before it's put on display. That's one reason for the hush-hush stuff."

Phil glanced around. "The other reason is that it's extremely valuable. Dr. Michaels has kept its arrival a tightly guarded secret."

Frank frowned. "I thought the cobra was the most deadly snake on earth."

Phil shook his head. "Cobras just have a bigger reputation. They're responsible for a lot of deaths in places like India and Malaysia."

"I'd say that's a good reason to be called deadly," Joe said.

Phil laughed and agreed. "Actually, Joe, people can survive cobra bites untreated, but no one has ever lived through a tiger-snake bite without immediate treatment. Its venom may be twenty-five times more powerful than a cobra's." He shook his head. "What's more, tiger snakes aren't shy, like most snakes. They'll stand their ground. Luckily, they're rare and don't live where there are many humans."

"So where is this killer snake?" asked Frank. "Do we get a chance to see him?"

Phil pulled a bronze-colored plastic card from his pocket. "This security pass opens the gate. Allow me."

Seconds later the lock was released, and Phil swung open the gate. The boys climbed back in the van and drove on to the employees' parking lot, where they pulled into an open spot.

Phil pointed to a small building on the grounds. "That's the security shack—they have alarms wired to sensors all around the zoo. You can't get by them without a pass." He patted his pocket. "The L-shaped building to the left is the lab. That's where we're going."

Frank mused, "Security here is something else! Why? Who'd steal anything from a zoo?"

"Some specimens are very valuable," Phil said, "although I think you'd have to be nuts to make off with an eighteen-foot python. Security's tight, but it's also pretty safe—you need a pass to get in, but an automatic eye lets you out." He grinned. "That's a good idea if you wander into the tiger cage."

Joe was staring across the nearly deserted parking lot. "Wow! A Pillari Four Hundred!" Frank and Phil followed his gaze to a sports car at the far end of the lot. Its flame red body gleamed.

"That's a custom-made, high-performance driving machine," Joe said with a low whistle.

"Nice," Frank agreed. "What's it worth, Mr. Car Nut?"

"Probably more than an average zoo employee earns," Joe said, his eyes fixed on the car.

"I'll say!" Phil said sourly. "What I make will barely cover the cost of that new computer system I need." He gestured to the car. "I've seen it before, but I don't think it belongs to anyone on the staff."

"Morning, Phil!" called a security man who was crossing the lot.

"Tom, meet my friends." Phil introduced the Hardys to Tom McGuire, a zoo security guard.

McGuire shook hands, then pulled a sheet from his clipboard. "You're on the approved list—and this is one short list!" He also opened an envelope to produce two cards similar to Phil's.

"Your passes," he explained, handing one to each Hardy. "Clip them on whenever you're in the lab." He turned to Phil. "By the way, you're supposed to report to the administrator."

5

Phil frowned. "Thanks, Tom. I'd better see what he wants. Can you show them around?"

"Sure—you're the only early arrivals."

McGuire and the Hardys watched as Phil hurried off, still frowning. The guard muttered, "Mad Michaels strikes again."

Frank looked startled. "Mad Michaels? You mean Dr. Michaels?"

"That's the one," McGuire said. "Phil and the mighty Michaels had a real go-round. The doc came down pretty hard on him."

"Why?" Joe asked as the boys followed McGuire in the direction of the lab.

"Phil was wiring something," explained Tom, "and he accidentally slipped a magnetic screwdriver into his pocket—the same one his security pass was clipped to. The magnetized tool erased the coding on the card. When Phil passed one of the sensors in the lab, the alarms went wild."

McGuire led the way to the snack bar. "We won't get into the lab for a while yet—not till they've got that new snake safely locked up. Would you boys like something to eat?"

"Well, I missed breakfast," Joe admitted. Soon he was munching on a hot dog with the works.

Frank made a gagging sound. "How can anyone eat a hot dog before ten?"

Joe ignored him. "So Phil erased his card? That sounds pretty harmless to me."

6

"Joe's right," Frank said. "Dr. Michaels's reaction does sound extreme."

Now they were strolling past a pool where some seals dashed after the fresh fish a zoo employee had tossed out. "I guess I didn't mention that the doc had a cobra out at the time, getting ready to milk it," McGuire said. "The alarm distracted him, and the snake almost nailed him."

"Whoa!" Joe said. "I've heard of milking cows, even goats—but how do you milk a cobra?"

"Very carefully!" Frank grinned. "Milking is a process for getting venom. I saw a film of it once. The snake's mouth is forced open, the fangs are pressed over a diaphragm, and venom is gathered in a vial."

"People actually do that for a living?" Joe shook his head in disbelief.

"It's pretty dangerous," McGuire agreed. "Maybe that's why the doc came unglued. He said he was going to fire Phil and see to it that he never worked for the zoo again."

Frank stopped by the tiger cage and watched the powerful animals pace back and forth. "It sounds as if you don't think much of Michaels."

"He's okay, I guess," answered Tom, "until you mess up. Then he's on you like feathers on a duck! I've seen the doc crawl all over a guard about nothing at all. He chews his own assistant out like the guy was a total idiot." McGuire grinned. "He even tried to throw Dr. Hagen out of the lab."

"Dr. Hagen? Who's that?" Joe asked.

"The zoo's physician. She's on staff at the University Medical Center and takes care of us, too—from claw scratches to fur allergies. She's a terrific doctor and a really nice woman."

They walked on. "Michaels could take lessons from her. The doc's brilliant, but he knows a lot more about handling snakes than people." Tom stopped to sip from his coffee cup. "One thing's certain—Harrod Michaels isn't the president of the Phil Cohen fan club."

"Maybe he cooled off by now," Joe said.

Tom shrugged. "He's not one to forgive and forget. I'm amazed he even let Phil bring you guys to view his snake. Considering how hush-hush this project is, that's a compliment." He glanced at his watch. "What's keeping Phil? It shouldn't take this long to draw a pink slip."

"You really think he's getting fired?" Frank glanced at his brother. "If Phil loses his job, he'll never get that new computer."

Joe nodded. "Poor Phil. Buying that system is all he's talked about for weeks."

They walked past a brown stone building. "Here's Administration—I'll go in and see."

The Hardys waited on the steps for Tom. Early zoo visitors were coming in by the time he reappeared. "Phil left here a while ago. Let's check the lab. Everything should be ready by now."

They cut through a heavily wooded area and found themselves in front of the lab.

"Give me your pass, Frank. I'll show you how to use it." Tom inserted Frank's card in a slot next to the door frame, and the door slid open.

The lab wasn't large, but it was arranged to make the most of every inch of space. Glass cases were stacked along the aisles, and the boys peered at the reptiles inside in fascination. In one case a timber rattler lay coiled, its tail buzzing an ominous warning. In another, a reptile spread its hood, revealing itself to be a cobra.

"We've had some run-ins with snakes," Frank said, staring around. "I don't think I'd like to spend my life around them."

As he spoke the snake in the cage next to his elbow hissed angrily and lunged at the glass.

"I know what you mean!" Joe laughed nervously and glanced around. "But where's Phil?"

Tom said, "I've been pulling overtime for this snake delivery, so I'd better check in. It was good meeting you. If I see Phil, I'll send him your way." He turned and walked briskly down an aisle and out of sight.

Frank frowned. "Phil was really hot to see this Australian snake. This is—" He was interrupted by a horrible scream.

9

"It came from down there," Joe said, running down an aisle that ended abruptly at a doorway. A sign above it read, Dr. Harrod Michaels.

"Dr. Michaels!" Frank called, pounding on the heavy door. There was no answer.

Joe spotted a slot next to the door and said, "Try your card, Frank."

Frank slipped the card in, but the door didn't budge. "Dr. Michaels!"

Frank shook his head at the ominous silence. "This door must have a different code—to keep out casual visitors like us."

Joe had already raced out to get help.

Two guards arrived, one with a master key. But the lock still didn't budge. "Bolt must be thrown," muttered the guard. He pounded on the door. "Dr. Michaels!" Then he shook his head. "It's no use, we'll have to break it down."

The security team and the Hardys put their shoulders to the door, but it still wouldn't move. One guard finally found a heavy crowbar. After tremendous effort they finally sprung the door open, tumbling into the room just as Phil panted up behind them.

"Phil! Where have you—" Joe began.

Phil brushed past him, then skidded to a halt. "Dr. Michaels!" he cried in alarm.

Michaels lay slumped over his desk. An open case bearing the official seal of Australia lay on the floor beside him—empty. A bloodred warn-

10

ing label, stenciled with a skull and crossbones, read, DANGER: VENOMOUS SNAKE.

Michaels's eyes were glazed, and his lips had a bluish tint. "Can you hear me?" Phil took the scientist's wrist. "Fast, erratic pulse—it looks like he might be paralyzed, too. Classic snakebite symptoms." He gulped, staring at the empty box. "There must be a snake loose in here!"

"The tiger snake!" murmured Frank. "The deadliest snake in the world."

In the uneasy silence that followed they could hear the whir of a faraway fan.

"We need help." Joe reached across the desk for the phone, but Phil's arm shot out, slamming him back. Joe's eyes blazed. "Phil! What—?"

Phil Cohen's eyes were fixed on a spot in the center of Michaels's desk. He pointed a finger.

Openmouthed, Joe stared, too.

The papers on top of Michaels's desk were moving.

2 Snakes on the Loose

Everyone in the room was spellbound by the movement on Michaels's desk. Then Frank glanced upward and laughed. "It's just a breeze," he said. "The ventilator is right above the desk."

Joe gave Phil a worried look. His friend was still shaken up. Phil's eyes darted around the office nervously, searching its corners.

"I'll get Mr. Fizer," a guard said to no one in particular. "And I'll ask one of our men outside to call for an ambulance."

"Mr. Fizer?" Frank repeated, looking at Phil as the guards ushered everyone out of the room.

"Fizer is Michaels's assistant," Phil answered. "He's basically a snake handler."

Joe put a hand on Phil's arm. "Where have you been?" he asked. "What's wrong?"

His friend shook the hand off, snapping, "Everything's wrong!" He took a deep breath.

"I lost my job. Ever since Dr. Michaels told me, I've just been walking and thinking."

Just then Grant Fizer arrived, with the ambulance crew at his heels. "Wait till I check the office," he warned them, staring at his boss's slumped body. "One snakebite victim is enough!"

Joe noted how professionally the tall, gaunt man with thinning dark hair went about his work. Using a six-foot-long, rubber-tipped snake hook, he carefully searched the room. "All clear," he announced. "If it was here, it's gone now."

"Gone?" Joe stepped into the office, followed by Frank and Phil. "How?"

Fizer shrugged. "Maybe Michaels left his door open and it slipped out. Snakes are superb escape artists. It could have crawled out right under your noses." He gave a thin smile. "Be glad it didn't bite anyone on the way out."

He tossed his stick into a corner. "Now it looks like we have a valuable and deadly snake running loose in the zoo. Purdy!" Fizer called to the security man at the door, "we've got to search for and find this snake before anyone else is hurt."

He glared at the guard. "Tell your people when they find it, stay clear. If you're bitten, you're dead. It just takes minutes." Fizer sighed. "I hate the idea of handling it alone, but I'm the only one here with enough experience."

13

Michaels was loaded on a stretcher, and Grant Fizer was handed a release form. After scrawling his signature, he folded the form and returned it to the medics, who wheeled Dr. Michaels away.

"Where will they take him?" Joe asked.

"University Medical Center," Fizer replied. "UMC's the only place around here set up to treat snakebite." He smiled wanly. "Luckily, it's less than two miles away. The doc'll be under medical care in a few minutes."

"Frank, will you drive me over there?" Phil asked. "I'd like to make sure . . ." He paused, then finished weakly, "Maybe we can help."

"Buck up," Fizer said. "He can't blame this on you." He saw them to the door. "As soon as things are organized, I'll be there myself."

They walked quickly to the van. "Weirder and weirder," Frank muttered as he slid behind the wheel. "Where's the snake? Michaels's office has no windows, and the door was locked on the inside. That snake has got to be in the lab."

"Maybe it drove off in that red sports car," Joe kidded. "I see it's gone."

"I'm serious," Frank said as they drove to the hospital. "Why was Michaels's door locked?"

"I noticed something stranger," Phil said as they pulled up by the hospital. "The office was really stuffy, and lab temperature is something scientists monitor carefully. The office should

14

have been the same as the rest of the lab, which was very comfortable."

"That stuff may be mysterious," Joe said, "but I think the missing snake tops the list."

Inside the hospital a nurse led them to the Intensive Care Unit, where a wiry woman with a thin, pale face and short gray hair stood in the entrance. Old-fashioned glasses perched precariously on the end of her nose, and she looked over the top of them as the three boys approached.

"Dr. Hagen?" Phil said.

The doctor peered at Phil. "Cohen, isn't it? Another burn?"

"I got burned when some solder spattered," Phil explained to the Hardys. "Dr. Hagen took care of me." He turned to the doctor, saying, "We came to see how Dr. Michaels was doing."

"I'd like an answer to that question, too," Grant Fizer said, joining the group.

The doctor shook her head. "It's too soon to tell. His condition is extremely serious."

"Can we talk with him?" Phil asked anxiously.

"We'd all like to talk with him," the doctor replied grimly. "Then we'd know what happened."

"What do you mean? It's snakebite!" Grant Fizer said.

Dr. Hagen nodded slowly. "Probably."

15

"Weren't there fang marks?" Phil asked.

Her face clouded. "He has a puncture here." She touched the base of her neck. "It resembles a snakebite, but there's only one wound."

"A snake with just one fang?" Joe suggested.

Hagen looked doubtful. "Snakes lose a fang now and then, but they grow back quickly."

"No way," Fizer stated. "We're very careful about new arrivals. They must be in perfect condition." The others looked at him questioningly. "Snakes have almost no antibodies," he explained. "A small cut could mean death by infection. So no snake would have been shipped missing a fang."

Dr. Hagen motioned them to follow her into her office. She sat down tiredly. "Grant, why would Michaels inspect a snake in his office?"

"Beats me! We have a special area for that purpose. Only a fool would handle a tiger snake alone." Fizer shook his head. "And the doc's no fool."

Hagen slipped off her glasses and rubbed her eyes. "And how on earth could he have been bitten on the neck?"

Frank nodded. "That's right—snakes strike downward, so how could it reach that high?"

"Maybe Dr. Michaels was kneeling to open the case when the snake bit him," Phil offered.

"That might explain it," Fizer agreed. "The snake's head must have been almost five feet above the ground. Ours is eight feet long." He shrugged. "Michaels is lucky. By rights, he should be dead. If not for his immunity, he would be."

Joe looked confused. "Immunity to snakebite?"

Dr. Hagen rose and began pacing. "It's possible to build a mild immunity to venom. Michaels spent months on it to guard against this very kind of accident. You inject small amounts of venom into the bloodstream, then gradually increase the dosage with each treatment."

"So Dr. Michaels will recover?" asked Frank.

"Who knows?" Worry lines creased the doctor's brow. "So far he's not reacting properly. I've treated him for snakebite before, but this time he's unresponsive." She slapped her desktop in frustration. "Why?"

"Can't you give him antivenom?" Joe asked.

"*Antivenin,*" Dr. Hagen corrected. "If I was certain that the tiger snake bit him, I would. But the wrong antivenin will kill him. I'd rather see the snake first—and see if it has one fang."

Grant Fizer rose to his feet. "I'm going back to help with the search. Keep me posted, will you, doctor?"

Hagen nodded as Fizer strode briskly off.

"Guy knows a lot about snakes," Joe said.

"He's very dedicated," Dr. Hagen agreed, then added, "and very different from Dr. Michaels. Mr. Fizer is quiet, almost cold, like his snakes, while Michaels is temperamental." She

17

smiled at Phil. "But that's not news to you, is it?"

Phil shook his head.

The phone rang, and Dr. Hagen plucked it from its cradle. She listened a moment, said, "I understand. Yes, thank you," and hung up. "That was the ICU. He's worse. I must go now."

Joe glanced at his watch. "It's past noon. Let's grab a bite in the cafeteria." He glanced at Dr. Hagen. "If we can help, let us know."

Hagen nodded as she hurried away.

The boys headed for the hospital cafeteria and got some sandwiches. They had just finished eating when Dr. Hagen hurried up to their table.

"Dr. Michaels is failing," she said bluntly. "He needs antivenin now, but we haven't gotten it from the zoo. It seems everyone is out looking for the snake. I need someone to run over and pick it up for me."

"No problem!" Frank said, shoving his chair back. "We'll be back in a couple of minutes."

Hagen scrawled something on a pad. "Show this to whoever's in charge of the storage unit."

"Let's go!" Frank said. They ran for the van and soon arrived at the zoo. Staff members and guards seemed to be everywhere.

"Hey, they shut down the security system," Phil said as they passed the gate.

"Why would they do that?" wondered Joe.

18

"With all those people moving around," Phil said, "maybe they're afraid of false alarms."

He scanned the crowd. "There's Tom. He'll have a key to get to the antivenin stores." Phil waved to catch the guard's attention.

"No time to visit," Tom said. "We have some major problems right now."

Frank gave him the slip from Dr. Hagen. "Dr. Michaels needs antivenin right away."

McGuire glanced at the note. "This way. We store both venom and antivenin in a special room next to the doc's office." He led them to the lab but stopped dead before an open door.

The boys looked over his shoulder. Racks for vials of antivenin and venom stood empty. Tom McGuire groaned, "More thefts! What next?"

"More thefts?" Frank said in surprise. "What are you talking about?"

"The zoo's keeping it quiet," Tom said. "We're not just searching for the tiger snake— a number of other snakes are missing. Someone has ripped off some very deadly merchandise."

Phil said, "We need to call Dr. Hagen right away! Dr. Michaels's life depends on it!"

Frank nodded. "You're right, Phil. Tom, can we use the phone in Dr. Michaels's office?"

"Help yourself. I have to find Mr. Fizer right away. He needs to know about this."

As Frank spoke on the phone Joe prowled around the office. Books lined the walls. A

19

computer sat in one corner. The reptile case, used to ship the tiger snake, stood empty by the desk. As Joe moved the box to read the label a neatly folded bit of colored paper caught his eye. He unfolded it, to find a ticket stub that read:

ADMIT ONE: MUSTANGS VS. TI——
OCTOBER 1—TITAN STADIUM, ME——

It was a New Jersey pro football ticket.

Joe glanced over as Frank slammed the phone down. His brother's face was grim. "Dr. Hagen called the Reptile Research Institute in L.A., the nearest place that has tiger snake antivenin. A jet's flying it here."

"What about Michaels?" Phil asked anxiously.

"She hopes she can keep him alive that long. Right now he's on a life-support machine." Frank gazed around the office. "Look at this place. No family photos, no personal stuff, just scientific equipment. He must live for snakes."

"Not quite," Joe said, handing over the stub.

Frank shrugged. "A wrinkled ticket stub. So?"

"Nothing, I guess. It just doesn't match the rest of the stuff in this office."

Frank shrugged. "Litter. Someone missed the trash, or it fell from someone's pocket, or—"

"What are you doing here?" Fizer's voice

demanded from the doorway. "Oh, it's you guys." His voice softened. "McGuire told me about the theft. As if I didn't have enough headaches!"

The snake handler started chewing a stick of gum. He looked at the boys, then held out the pack. "Want one? I gave up smoking recently." He grinned sheepishly. "So I need a new bad habit."

The boys declined the gum, and Fizer replaced the pack in his pocket, fiddling absently with the empty gum wrapper. "Any word on the doc?"

He listened grimly as Frank reported what Dr. Hagen had said. "Still unconscious? That's bad. I hope he makes it. He's a great snake man."

"Have you worked with him long?" Joe asked.

Fizer shrugged. "A few months. Why?"

"Maybe you could tell us something." Joe held out the ticket stub. "Do you know where this might have come from?"

Fizer stopped chewing and peered at the stub. "It must be Michaels's, I guess. Look, guys, excuse me. I've got to get back to work."

He paused, then added, "You guys had better turn in those passes. We have big problems here, and I don't want any more accidents." A voice in the hall called him, and he hurried away.

Tom McGuire stuck his head in. "Fellas, I'm supposed to ask you to leave."

21

"Any word on the antivenin?" Joe asked.

"Nope," Tom replied glumly. "Bill Purdy, our security chief, phoned the cops. They'll be here to investigate—and to help with the search." He put his hand on Phil's shoulder. "Phil, stay in touch. Gotta run, guys!" And he hurried away.

Frank looked at Phil, full of concern. His friend was staring blankly at the bookcase. "Hey, Phil, were your folks expecting you home any special time?"

"No, I have the house to myself. They're away, taking a sort of second honeymoon."

"Come on and hang out with us for a while," Joe suggested.

They were just leaving the office when two workers burst in. "Excuse me," one said. "I need the phone." He brushed past while his partner leaned in the doorway, panting.

"What's up?" Joe inquired.

"We may have found a snake," the man said.

"The tiger snake?" Frank asked hopefully.

The man shook his head. "Don't know."

"Where? In the woods?" Phil asked.

"Nope," came the reply. "Some woman drove up from a laundromat about six blocks from here. She saw a kid fooling with a big snake behind the building. Word's getting out about why we evacuated the zoo this morning." He paused, then added, "They tried to hush it up, but there's no way you can keep something like

22

that quiet." He pointed back outside. "Anyway, this woman came to the gate babbling about this kid."

"Was he bitten?" Frank exclaimed.

"We don't know. Max"—he gestured to the man talking urgently on the phone—"is calling Purdy right now to get a team over there to check it out." He shook his head. "Half a dozen snakes loose, and the temperature is going down to the mid-fifties tonight."

"What's that got to do with it?" Joe asked.

The man's face was grim. "Snakes are cold-blooded. They'll be looking for warm places to hide. Places like houses—"

"Or laundromats," the other worker added as he hung up. "They're on their way, even Mr. Fizer. While I was talking, another call came in from the same laundry." The man's face was pale. "Someone else saw the snake and got a better look at it. They say it's about eight feet long."

Phil gasped, and Frank and Joe looked at each other with alarm.

The tiger snake was eight feet long!

3 Phil Is Accused

Phil glanced around wildly. "Isn't there anything we can do?"

Max shook his head, then glanced at his watch. "Fizer will be there by now. They'll call when they know something." Time seemed to drag, but finally the phone rang, and Max snatched it up. He listened silently, then grinned. "Jake, huh? Best news I've had all day. Thanks, Larry." He replaced the receiver slowly.

"Well?" Joe demanded impatiently.

Max grinned. "It *was* one of our snakes at the launderette. But it was Jake, so there was no harm done."

"Jake?" Frank repeated. "Who's Jake?"

"Jake's an eight-foot-long king cobra."

"A king cobra? In a launderette?" Phil cut in. "Is the kid . . . did he . . . ?"

Max smiled. "Whoever that kid is, he was

24

born under a lucky star. Jake was given to us a while back by a circus. He was one of their acts." Max grinned. "He's defanged. He's big and ugly—"

"But harmless," his partner finished. "We lucked out this time."

Max frowned. "Yeah, this time. Next time, though . . ." He didn't need to finish the statement. Everyone in the room knew that their luck wouldn't last forever.

They all started to leave the office, only to find the doorway blocked by the stocky form of Ezra Collig. Bayport's chief of police, Collig often encountered the Hardys as they worked on cases. He definitely wasn't happy to see them. "I'm supposed to see the zoo's snake expert," he growled. "Instead, I find you two here."

He might have gone on, but Grant Fizer came into the room with Bill Purdy close on his heels. The snake handler glared at the uniformed police officers in the lab. Then he turned to the chief. "What's going on here? Who are you?"

"I'm Chief Collig," Collig snapped, annoyed by Fizer's challenging tone. "Who are you?"

"Grant Fizer—I'm in charge here. What are you doing butting in?"

"Excuse me, Mr. Fizer," Purdy interrupted, "but I thought we'd better call in the police."

"You did, did you?" Fizer exploded. "You think a bunch of dumb flatfeet will do better than our own people?"

Purdy's eyes flashed angrily as he responded through clenched teeth. "We've had a theft, sir—and a very dangerous situation."

As Fizer started to make an angry retort Chief Collig bellowed, "Knock it off!" He pointed at Purdy. "Now you, sir, fill me in on what's happening here. And you," Collig continued, pointing at Grant Fizer, "keep still until I have the facts."

The Hardys listened closely as Bill Purdy quickly filled Collig in on Michaels's accident and the missing snakes. Collig asked tiredly, "Some snake venom is missing, too?"

"Venom as well as antivenin," Purdy said.

"Plus a half dozen reptiles. I'd call this a *very* dangerous situation," Collig said. "Right now we don't know if the snakes have been taken from the grounds or let loose somewhere. And I haven't the foggiest idea who would steal poisonous snakes in the first place."

"What I can't figure out is how the snakes were taken from the premises," added Purdy.

"A very good question. How were the reptiles stolen, and what do you intend to do about it, Chief Collig?" a strange voice demanded. Every eye was drawn to the back of the room.

Collig glared at the speaker. "Who are you?" he demanded.

A well-dressed, athletic-looking man with bright red hair stepped out of the crowd. "My name's Bradshaw, Tad Bradshaw. You may have

26

heard of me. I'm a stringer for some news services in New York, and it looks to me as if you have quite a news story here."

Collig's eyes narrowed. "Bradshaw." He scratched his head. "Are you the same Bradshaw who did that story about unsafe plastic toys?" The man nodded. "And reported on the toxic waste dumping in Barmet Bay?"

"Yes, that's me." Bradshaw grinned. "Right now I'm the reporter who's writing about the snakes missing from the Bayport Zoo. Those snakes are loose in town—killer snakes. People have a right to know how you intend to protect them." Bradshaw thrust a tape recorder microphone beneath Collig's nose.

"We . . . ah, that is . . . I, um . . ." the surprised cop sputtered, his ruddy face turning even redder. Finally, he took a deep breath, glared at the newsman, and growled, "We'll do everything in our power to recover the missing reptiles. At this point, we have no hard evidence indicating that venomous snakes are loose in the city. Someone may be holding them somewhere, this may just be a bizarre prank, or—"

"No hard evidence?" the reporter repeated incredulously. "Just what do you consider hard evidence? A tiger snake, the most deadly snake on earth, is missing, and a man's in the hospital. You just heard a snake was found in a launderette—by a six-year-old kid!" He continued coldly, "What's it going to take, Chief

Collig? Does a little boy have to die before you'll consider it 'hard evidence'?"

Collig sputtered like a lawnmower with fouled plugs. But before he could come up with an answer, the reporter yanked the microphone away.

"You!" Bradshaw turned on Bill Purdy. "You're chief of security at the zoo, right?"

Purdy nodded uncomfortably. "Then you're the one responsible for these reptiles being loose, right?" Looking trapped, Purdy backed away from the microphone. Bradshaw pursued him, firing questions like a machine gun.

As they moved off into a corner of the office Collig breathed a sigh of relief. "Who let him in here?" he demanded. When no one answered, Collig shrugged and began snapping orders to his men, organizing a search for the missing snakes.

Frank threw Joe a puzzled look. "I don't get it. Who'd steal half a dozen deadly snakes, the venom, and antivenin? It doesn't make sense!"

Joe shrugged. "Good question. Here's another: How'd they do it?"

A deep humming sound caught their attention. A breeze brushed Dr. Michaels's desk. Frank caught a loose paper as it skittered across the desktop, then paused. He looked up, stared at the ceiling, then snapped his fingers. "That's it!" he exclaimed.

Joe followed his brother's gaze. A moment

28

later, he cried, "Of course! Locked door, no window, it's the only possible explanation."

"What are you two babbling about?" Collig demanded, his attention drawn by the boys' exclamations.

"We know how the theft was pulled off," Frank replied, pointing to the large vent above Michaels's desk. "It's the only explanation."

Without hesitation, Collig turned to one of his men. "Rogers, check out that vent."

"M-me, Collig?"

"Yes, you!" Collig growled, then he eyed the suddenly pale man curiously. "What's the problem?"

"Chief, I have this thing about snakes. I mean, shouldn't we let an expert check it out? There could be a snake waiting in there—"

"Rogers, check that vent out now. That's an order!"

Rogers nodded miserably, then left to locate a screwdriver and stepladder. He returned shortly, armed with a flashlight and a tool belt. A zoo employee came behind him carrying a ladder. Rogers gave two quick twists of the screwdriver, and the hinged vent grate swung open. Collig stared at the cover for a moment, then muttered to Frank, "Nice theory, Hardy, but how could a crook open that? The screw heads are on this side."

"Look again, Chief Collig," Joe answered, pointing. "Those aren't screws, they're latches.

29

Anyone inside could simply turn the latch with his fingers or a screwdriver and open the vent."

Collig stared at the hardware on the vent cover and finally nodded. "It wouldn't be hard to do, I guess. Check out that shaft, Rogers," he ordered.

The frightened police officer hesitated, but a growl from Collig spurred him to action. He poked his head inside the air shaft, paused, then stepped to the top of the ladder, half of his body now in the shaft. A muffled cry of surprise made everyone in the room jump.

Officer Rogers slowly backed down from the hole. As he turned to face Collig the Hardys saw that he was gingerly holding something with a handkerchief. It was a large, black-handled screwdriver. "Someone's been in there, all right. There are fresh marks in the dust, and this screwdriver was lying in the shaft just a few feet from the vent."

"Let's see that thing," Collig said, plucking the tool from the officer's shaky hand, being careful to use the handkerchief to avoid erasing any fingerprints. Collig inspected the handle, then handed the tool back to Rogers.

"This is evidence, Rogers. Turn it over to our lab people to check for fingerprints." He turned to Fizer, who'd been silent throughout the entire operation. "That screwdriver, do you recognize it?"

Fizer shook his head angrily. "Why should I? A screwdriver's a screwdriver."

Collig shook his head. "Not this one. This tool has someone's initials etched in the handle."

"Oh? Whose initials?" Fizer demanded.

Collig shrugged. "I don't know. Anyone working for you with the initials P.C.?"

Fizer's mouth opened, but before he could say anything there was a commotion from the back of the room. A figure darted from the doorway and started to run down the aisle of the outer lab.

Collig shouted to his men in the outer lab, "Someone grab that guy! Stop him." They heard sounds of running, a quick scuffle, then silence. A moment later, two officers entered the cramped office leading a figure between them.

Chief Collig took the screwdriver from Rogers's hand once more and inspected the engraving. "P.C.," he mused, then he glared at the frightened figure held between two of his officers.

"P.C.," he repeated as Frank and Joe looked on in shock. "Phil Cohen."

4 Panic in Bayport

Phil Cohen looked dazed as Officer Rogers took him by the arm. "Will you come along peacefully, or do I have to arrest you?" the police officer said as the Hardys looked on in disbelief.

"Phil, what's going on?" asked Frank.

"I haven't done anything," Phil answered.

Chief Collig held up the screwdriver. "Yours?" he asked. Phil nodded miserably. Collig sighed and said, "Take him in for questioning."

Frank was horrified. "Chief Collig, you can't believe Phil had anything to do with this."

"What I believe doesn't matter," the chief replied coldly. "It was your idea to check the vent, and we found Phil's screwdriver in it. That tool is evidence that points to your friend."

"But he was with us!" Joe blurted.

"Was he with you when Michaels screamed?"

"Well, no, he was in the Administration—"

Collig's voice grew hard. "Oh? Were you with him?" There was a long silence. "I've known Phil for years." He sighed. "But until I have proof he's not involved, it's my job to take him in."

Joe started to protest, but Frank stopped him. "Come on, Joe, this won't help. Let's call Dad. Maybe he can do something."

Three hours later, Fenton Hardy and attorney Tyrus Reeves had secured Phil's release. The young man was sullenly silent as they sat down at a table in a diner near the courthouse.

"You're in trouble, Phil," Reeves said bluntly. "The evidence against you is circumstantial, but it may be enough to convict you."

"But—" Phil protested.

Reeves held up his hand. "Let me finish. The police are busy building a case against you. And you didn't help yourself by running away."

Phil stared around wildly. "Come on," he said pleadingly. "You know I didn't steal those snakes."

Fenton Hardy shifted uncomfortably. "Phil, why *did* you run?"

Phil hung his head. "I recognized my screwdriver, and I could see what was coming next." He shrugged. "I guess I just panicked."

Frank reached over and put a hand on his friend's arm. "No one here thinks you stole anything, but it's Mr. Reeves's job to let you know how things stand."

"Phil, how did that screwdriver get into that ventilation shaft?" Joe asked.

Phil shrugged. "Who knows? It should have been in my toolbox. I know I had it when I was building the display case." He sighed. "I wish I'd never taken that job!"

Fenton Hardy frowned. "Tyrus didn't tell you the worst of it, Phil."

"The worst of it? How can it get worse?"

"If Dr. Michaels dies, it changes everything," Fenton Hardy said quietly.

"It's like this," Tyrus Reeves explained. "If he dies and they prove he was injured during a criminal act, you could be tried for murder."

"Murder!" Joe gasped.

Phil put his head in his hands.

Fenton Hardy placed a hand on Phil's shoulder. "Phil, we'll do all we can to help you, but you've got to keep a level head."

Reeves said, "Chief Collig has gotten a warrant to search your home." He gave Phil a hard look. "He won't find anything, will he?"

Phil stared at the attorney, then snapped, "Sure! I'm Bayport's biggest criminal! There are bodies in my basement and snakes in my garage! Want to accuse me of anything else?" Phil sprang to his feet, knocking over his chair. "I don't need this. I didn't steal anything! If you don't believe me, that's tough! Now leave me alone!"

"Wait, Phil—" Fenton Hardy began, but the

Hardys' friend had already stormed out the door.

"Forget it, Dad," said Joe. "He isn't himself right now."

Reeves stood up. "I have to go." He shook his head as he left. "I'm worried about that boy. He'll make himself more trouble."

Frank turned to his father. "We appreciate your help, Dad."

"I wish there was more I could do," answered Fenton, "but I have a case, and I just can't get free." He drummed his fingers on the table absentmindedly. "Unfortunately, Phil has a motive—the fight he had with Michaels. And he plainly had the opportunity—all that time he was missing."

He looked up. "But he doesn't have the snakes. You boys need to concentrate on finding the snakes or someone who had a better motive or opportunity than Phil." He smiled. "What's needed is plain old detective work."

Frank and Joe grinned as their father added confidently, "You'll figure it out." Then his face clouded. "Be careful. I have a feeling this case will be more complicated than it seems right now."

For the moment following his words, a chill hung in the air.

The next morning, Joe flung the morning paper down on the table. "Phil's made the front page," he declared. The headline read, "Bayport Youth Implicated in Snake Theft." Beneath it in smaller letters it said, "Killer Snakes Stalk City."

Frank Hardy looked up from his breakfast and scowled. "What garbage!" Then he sighed. "The trouble is, we have no leads. None, that is, that don't point directly to Phil! Worse yet, the way Phil's acting could cause even more problems."

"I know." Joe looked uncomfortable. "Frank, I don't like to say it, but do you think there's a possibility Phil could actually be guilty?"

Frank stared glumly across the breakfast table and nodded slightly. "The thought has run through my mind," he admitted. "We know how badly he wanted that new computer system. But Phil's our friend. If he says he's innocent, I believe him. We have to find out who's behind this!"

Joe nodded. "I wish I knew where he went. I tried calling his home, but there's no answer." He grinned. "Let's cruise past his place."

"We'll take some friends, too," Frank added. "He can use all the support he can get right now."

Joe grinned. "I'll call Iola and Chet, you call Callie." His face was determined as he picked up the phone. "We'll clear Phil of this yet!"

A half hour later, Callie Shaw, Frank's pretty blond girlfriend, leaned over the passenger seat

36

of the Hardys' van. "I saw the paper. What the article says about Phil is awful."

Iola Morton, Joe's girlfriend, nodded. "I heard the story on the radio. The announcer said he was suspected of turning a bunch of snakes loose in town." Her normally bright eyes darkened. "I've never seen Phil act the way you described. It sure doesn't sound like the Phil I know!"

Frank eased the van into a spot in front of Phil's house. Three squad cars were parked in the driveway, and police seemed to be everywhere. A crowd of curious passersby had formed.

Chet Morton, Iola's brother, had just finished the last bit of his fast-food breakfast. "Man," he exclaimed, "look at all those people! Phil's famous!"

The group piled out of the van just as Officer Con Riley walked across the lawn to meet them. Riley was a longtime friend who had worked on many cases with the Hardys. His face was grim as he asked, "Have you seen Phil?"

"No," Frank replied. "Why? What's happening?"

Riley pointed to two men carrying a large case from Phil's basement. "That's what's happening."

"What's in the case, Officer Riley?" Iola asked.

Riley's face was expressionless as he replied,

"Two of the biggest cobras I've ever seen."

"Cobras!" Chet exclaimed. "Here?" Chet looked around nervously, as though more snakes might be lurking on Phil's trampled lawn.

"They were hidden in Phil's basement," explained Officer Riley.

"And they're definitely from our collection at the zoo," a voice behind them spat.

The boys turned to find Grant Fizer behind them, his face flushed with anger. He handed Riley a neatly folded piece of paper. "That's a list of eight snakes—you'll find the description of the two cobras there."

His hands clenched. "This is criminal! Those snakes have been treated shamefully. We'll be lucky if they don't die." He waved his fists angrily. "People are so stupid! They treat reptiles as threats instead of the wonderful animals they really are."

He hovered over the case with the cobras. "Do you know how people view these rare creatures? They see them as snakeskin purses and shoes! Well, I think the person who stole them is far more dangerous than these cobras are. I want Phil Cohen behind bars, and I want the three snakes still missing back!"

"Hey, wait a minute!" Frank snapped. "Are you accusing Phil of taking those snakes?"

Fizer poked a stiff finger at Frank's chest. "That's not my job," he snapped. "I just look after the zoo's reptiles. But I do know that your friend and Michaels had an argument over Cohen's incompetence. Now Michaels is in the hospital, and stolen snakes turn up at Cohen's house. What does that say to you?" Before anyone could answer, he turned and stalked away.

Joe looked stunned. "Talk about fanatics!"

Chet changed the subject by gesturing toward the people gathering on the sidewalk. "Look at the crowd."

Officer Riley grimaced. "We've sent them away twice, but they keep coming back. Your friend's case has created a lot of interest."

"Con, I'd like to look around Phil's house," Frank said.

The detective shook his head slowly. "Sorry, Frank. You know as well as I do I can't allow you inside with an investigation in progress."

"But—"

"I'm sorry," Riley said firmly. "The answer is no. But if we find out anything, I'll pass the information along."

As the police officer walked away Chet said, "Maybe we can find a clue *outside* Phil's place."

Joe brightened. "Yeah! Phil's been framed. There's no way he brought those snakes here. Maybe whoever did left some traces."

They scoured the area but found nothing. Any

clues that might have been there had long since been trampled by the crowd. Finally, Callie groaned, "It's no use. There's nothing here."

"You're right," Joe said, leaning against the car parked in front of the van. "But we have to clear Phil!" He glanced at Frank. "I'd like another look at Michaels's office."

"Why?" Frank asked.

"Because no one actually entered the air shaft to follow the trail. Maybe there's a clue there." Joe grinned and said, "What's the first thing Dad ever taught us?"

Frank grinned and recited, "Ask questions. Then, if all else fails, ask more questions."

Chet pulled a package of peanuts from his pocket, popping a few in his mouth. "Questions? You want questions? I've got plenty. How many people are involved? How'd they get in? From the roof? From the lab? How'd they get the snakes out? Why are some loose? Did they escape, or were they set free?" He grinned. "I should have been a game-show host."

Iola poked Chet in the ribs and giggled. "No way. Not everyone has a wide-screen TV."

Chet laughed. "But you have to admit, they're good questions."

"And we don't have an answer for a single one of them," Frank said grimly. "Joe's right. The investigation at the zoo wasn't thorough. A trip to Michaels's office is definitely in order."

The five friends were about to leave when

suddenly they heard an angry sound rising from the crowd gathered in front of Phil's house. It was an ugly, animal noise that made Frank's skin crawl. "What's going on?" he asked.

"Hey, look!" Callie said urgently, pointing down the street. A tall figure was striding toward them, dressed in a light windbreaker—a windbreaker exactly like the one Phil had been wearing when the boys last saw him.

"It's Phil!" Iola said excitedly.

Suddenly, a voice from the crowd shouted, "There he is! That's the guy! Get him!"

A roar went up as the crowd surged toward the figure like a wave. They watched in horror as the figure stopped and stared, took a faltering step backward, then turned and started to run. Before he'd gone a dozen feet, the mob was upon him.

"Frank, we have to help him!" Callie said.

"Where are the cops?" Chet demanded.

As if they'd heard him, police burst from the house and ran toward the crowd. Frank realized the mob was out of control. "Come on! We have to get Phil away from there!"

They rushed toward the angry people swarming around Phil. Frank pulled one man away from the fringe of the crowd and shouted in his face, "What's wrong with you? What are you doing?"

"He's trying to kill us!" The man took a wild swing. Frank ducked, shot out a leg, and tripped

41

the man onto the grass. Behind him he heard Joe struggling with someone, and Chet's shout told him his friend was busy, too.

Frank bent down and grabbed the man's collar. "Go home!" he said sharply. "Get out of here!" The man looked confused for a moment, then ashamed. He pushed Frank's hands away and dashed off.

Frank turned and found Callie and Iola beside him. The police were restoring order, and as the crowd began to thin out Joe and Chet joined them.

Finally it was over. Frank and Joe looked around Phil's lawn tiredly. It was empty once again—except for one still and bloody figure lying on the ground. A figure wearing a tattered, bloody windbreaker just like Phil Cohen's.

5 An Ill Wind for Joe

Joe and Frank dashed over to the silent figure as an ambulance pulled up along the curb. Two paramedics leaped out and gently rolled the man over. His face was cut and bruised—but it wasn't Phil Cohen's face! He was a total stranger. Joe shuddered. "They beat up the wrong guy!"

The man opened his eyes and tried to sit up. The medics loaded him onto the stretcher, assuring the Hardys he would be all right. The stranger gazed up at Joe's face and uttered just one word before the ambulance door closed: "Why?"

Con Riley walked up and stood quietly for a moment. Finally he said, "We have an APB—an all-points bulletin—out on Phil."

He stared intently at the group. "For Phil's sake, if you find him before we do, get him to turn himself in!"

43

"I still think we'll find some answers at the zoo," Joe said vehemently. "We have to get back into that lab and look around. There must be something we've overlooked. There must be!"

"I hate to rain on your parade, Joe, but I don't think the zoo's going to let you waltz in and search their facilities for clues that will help the guy suspected of stealing their snakes," Chet commented dryly.

Frank sighed. "Chet's right, Joe. It's a good idea, but we'll never get away with it in broad daylight." A grin spread across his face. "So—"

"Let's go after dark!" Callie finished with a laugh. "Honestly, Frank, you're so predictable!"

"Hey, wait a minute," Frank protested. "If we get caught—"

"Frank Hardy, if you're about to say we can't come, you can save your breath!" Iola said firmly. "Phil's our friend, too, and five sets of eyes are better than two!"

Frank threw up his hands. "Okay, I give up. We'll meet tonight about eight." He shrugged. "Who knows, maybe we can share a cell with Phil."

The boys spent the rest of the day checking Phil's usual hangouts, but they found no clues to his whereabouts. By the time they'd eaten dinner they were eager to get to the zoo.

At eight o'clock they picked up Chet, Iola, and Callie and parked the van among the trees that lined the drive into the zoo. Luckily none of

44

the guards had remembered to collect their security passes the day before, and the codes still opened the gates. On foot the five friends slipped through the darkness to the lab.

In front of the entrance, they paused. Frank whispered, "This is the place."

"It looks deserted," Callie said nervously.

"Not surprising," Joe told her. "Both the day and night crews were called in for the search. Anyone still on duty is probably searching for the snakes that are still missing."

"Don't get overconfident," Frank warned. "Security's tight in this place, and we're going to have to fool it. When we go in, stay real close together. We only have two passes, but if we stay close, I'm hoping the sensors will simply think we're two very large people."

"Make that three large people, Frank." Callie laughed. "You forgot Chet went off his diet."

"It's my civic duty," Chet explained. "I support our local businesses, and when that fifty-five-flavor ice cream place opened—"

"Shh!" Frank cautioned, laughing in spite of himself. The heavy door slid open when he inserted his card. There were no alarms or sirens. Frank sighed in relief. Either his theory was correct or the security system was still shut down.

Bunched together, they slipped down the silent aisles and into Michaels's office. The broken door had not yet been repaired. Joe soon found a switch, and the office was bathed in stark fluorescent light.

"Well, we're in," Frank announced. "The security checkpoints are in the lab, not in here, so we don't have to stay so close to each other."

"Whew! That's a relief," Chet said.

"Oh, I don't know." Iola grinned, still clinging to Joe's arm. "I kind of enjoyed it."

Joe turned beet red and muttered, "Let's start looking for clues."

He pointed to the vent, which hung open just as Officer Rogers had left it. "They found Phil's screwdriver near the entrance of the vent. As far as we know, they never looked any farther. I want to know what's there."

"Meanwhile," Frank said, "we'll go over this office with a fine-tooth comb. Phil's freedom depends on us. Joe, why don't you and Iola search the shaft?"

Chet and Frank boosted the pair up, one at a time. Inside the shaft Joe fumbled in his pocket and produced a penlight. Then he and Iola started down the narrow steel tunnel. It was eerie. A faint breeze whispered past them, and they dimly heard sounds echoing up and down the corridor. Joe panned his light back and forth, following the scuff marks that indicated someone had, indeed, crawled this way recently.

Iola stuck close to him, silently peering over

his shoulder. "Joe, I don't think I like this place much," Iola whispered, then she gasped as a pit opened before them. "What is that?"

"The main ventilation shaft, I think," Joe replied. "It runs from the roof to the floor." He hesitated, studying the scene below him. "But this one goes even farther. Look." He shone the light down on the squared hole, revealing a jungle of pipes and conduits below.

"Those must be the heating and cooling ducts for the entire zoo down there," said Iola. "The zoo must have a large tunnel system below ground for that sort of thing."

Joe nodded. "I wonder which direction we should go. Did the thieves come from above or below?"

Iola tapped his shoulder and whispered, "Look above us, Joe. I see the sky."

"I see something else, too. Fresh marks on the metal. Our crooks came from the roof."

"There's a big fan up there," Iola said.

Joe nodded as he remembered the paper that had blown across Michaels's desk, leading to the discovery of the vent. The fan had caused that breeze. He said, "Hold the light. I'm going up there."

"Be careful," Iola murmured.

Joe braced his back against one wall of the shaft, his legs against the opposite wall, and worked his way up by sliding his back up a few

47

inches, then walking his legs up. He was soon positioned directly below the fan.

Its blades caught the gleam of the penlight Iola held below him. They twirled softly, propelled by the evening breeze. He placed his arm between the blades and they stopped, but Joe was unpleasantly surprised to learn how much force the freewheeling fan carried. That had hurt!

Joe grasped a bar welded to the metal wall above the fan and pulled himself past the huge blades. A heavy grate was above him. Through it, he could see the stars. He pushed against the grate, but it didn't budge.

"Iola, see if you can shine the light on the grate up here," Joe called down.

Iola adjusted the tiny beam and called up, "How's that?"

"Great!" came Joe's muffled reply. "The edges of the grate are scratched, and the metal's bright where the paint's been scraped away. Someone's definitely been up here recently."

"Can you remove the grate?" called Iola.

He reached up with one hand for the latches that held the grate in place. "I wish I'd brought a screwdriver. I can't budge these latches with my fingers."

"I'll crawl back and get one," Iola offered.

"Hang on," Joe said. "There's a screwdriver blade on my pocketknife. Maybe that will work."

48

Slowly Joe worked his knife out of his pocket. His legs were propped against one wall of the shaft, his back wedged against the one opposite, and only the powerful muscles of his legs and back held him steady against the metal. Already his legs felt the first twinges of cramps. Finally he clasped the knife in his hand, and he quickly pried the screwdriver blade open.

Gripping the knife, Joe attacked the latches. Soon it became obvious why the crooks had used one of Phil's heavy-duty tools. The pocket-knife blade was too light for the heavy latches. After a few tries, Joe realized he was more likely to break his pocketknife blade than he was to turn the latches. With a sigh, he called down, "It's no use. My blade's too light to turn these things. We'll have to get a screwdriver."

"No problem." Iola's voice echoed up to him. "I'll go back and get one. It'll just take—"

The rest of her words were drowned out by a loud electrical click and the hum of electricity being fed to a heavy-duty motor.

"Joe!" Callie screamed. "Get out of there!"

Too late! Joe watched in horror as the mighty blades beneath him began to spin, gaining speed with each turn. In seconds the fan, just inches away, was roaring at full speed. Joe realized he was in deep trouble. Those heavy blades would slice him to ribbons if he fell.

"Iola, get help!" he yelled over the roar of the

49

fan. "Hurry! I can't hold on much longer!" He listened for the girl's reply, but the noise from the fan was deafening.

Joe inched himself back up the shaft as close to the top as he could get. His legs were really beginning to cramp! He had to get the grating off now—it was the only way out! Using the tiny knife blades, he went to work again on the latches.

His legs burned and his back ached with strain. Gripping the pocket knife with sweating palms, he twisted. The latch moved a fraction. He twisted harder. Even above the roar of the fan, he could hear the snap of the tool breaking. Joe stared at the shortened stub of his pocket-knife as the broken blade bounced down the shaft and ricocheted through the fan blades with a deafening racket.

There was no escape! "Iola!" Joe cried. He tried to force his fingers through the holes in the grate to gain relief for his screaming back and leg muscles. But the holes were too small; he couldn't get his fingers through.

Then Joe felt himself beginning to slip. The fan's roar throbbed in his ears, and he could feel its suction. He tried to wedge himself tighter, but in the dim light from the night sky he could see his feet sliding slowly down the slick metal sides of the shaft.

Pain shot up and down his weakening legs. He had only seconds left before he dropped. He could feel the blades whipping at the back of his shirt. In desperation, he inched back up the shaft. But the effort cost too much.

Joe's legs started shaking uncontrollably. He began to slide.

In a moment, he was going to be chopped to bits!

6 A Box Full of Trouble

In Dr. Michaels's office, Frank, Callie, and Chet had been busy investigating everything from the empty snake container to possible messages on the computer printer. Their search only turned up a small bit of blank paper in the trash, carefully folded, just like the ticket stub.

"I sure hope Iola and Joe do better," Chet said. "We haven't had much luck here."

They all heard the faint hum and felt the cool breeze that followed it. Callie smiled. "That's better. It was getting stuffy in here." Suddenly a loud clang echoed down the air shaft.

"I think Joe and Iola are in trouble," Frank whispered. He stared at the vent worriedly.

Callie's eyes widened. "Oh, no! The fan is running, and that clang was something hitting the blades." She gripped Frank's arm. "Frank, we have to get them out of there!"

Frank started to call out but caught himself. A

shout would alert security, but what else could he do?

Suddenly Iola's pale face appeared in the vent. "Joe's trapped and needs help. We have to shut off the fan—now!"

Chet quickly helped Iola down, and then he boosted Frank up. As Frank pulled himself into the vent he called, "There has to be a switch for that fan. Find it! I'll see if I can help Joe."

"Take the flashlight, Frank." Iola passed it up and briefly described Joe's location.

As Frank disappeared down the shaft a frantic search began in the office. When they couldn't locate the switch immediately, Chet said, "Maybe it's outside the office. I'll look."

"No, Chet!" Iola cried. "You don't have a security pass. You'll trip the alarms." She was too late. As Chet stepped out the door alarms began to blare, drowning out the sound of the fan. He dashed back inside, but the damage was done.

"Found it!" Callie shouted, pointing to a switch next to the bookcase. She turned a dial, and the breeze died almost immediately. In the next second the blare of the alarms stopped and the sound of running feet began to echo from beyond the outer lab.

"I'll bet we have some explaining to do," Chet muttered.

A man in a guard's uniform appeared before him.

"Who are you, and what are you doing here?" he demanded in a gruff voice.

Chet shrugged and grinned sheepishly. "We just wanted to see the zoo, Officer."

As Frank crawled down the shaft Chet's voice echoed hollowly up to him. The steady wind in his face had died away—his friends must have found the switch, but had they been in time? He crawled faster. Soon he was at the lip of the vertical shaft.

"Joe," he whispered. No answer. "Joe, where are you?"

A soft groan issued from below him, and with the penlight Frank could make out the rumpled form of his brother lying at the bottom of the shaft. "Are you okay?" Another quiet groan answered him.

Frank worked his way down, and soon his feet rested on a large heating conduit running across the floor of the underground passage. Switching on the light, he muttered, "Joe?" There was no answer. Joe was sprawled in front of him, with a large bruise on his forehead. Frank gripped his brother's shoulders and shook him. "Joe, are you okay? Speak to me."

"If you don't stop shaking me, I'm not going to be okay," Joe grumbled.

Frank grinned. "I should've known. You only hit your head. Nothing vital's damaged."

Joe groaned and sat up. "Oh, yeah? I feel like

54

an entire football team has used me as a tackling dummy."

"What happened?"

"For a second, I thought I was going to be cat food. I slipped down, and the blades were coming closer, but the power was cut off just before I fell."

"Iola told us you were in trouble," Frank said, grinning. "I think you owe her."

Joe chuckled in spite of himself. "Well, that's one thank-you I won't mind delivering."

Frank gazed up the shaft and shuddered. The fan was turning slowly in the evening breeze. "You were lucky, Joe."

"I wonder if the thieves knew about that fan," said Joe.

"They must have," answered Frank.

Joe nodded, then winced. He struggled to his feet and leaned against a heating duct. "The switch must be in Dr. Michaels's office," he said. "That means someone had to shut the fan off for the thieves. Someone with access to that office."

"And someone had to turn it on again when they were safely gone," Frank said thoughtfully, "because it was working shortly after we found Dr. Michaels. Is it possible that Dr. Michaels is one of the crooks?"

Even in the darkness, Frank could sense Joe's startled look. "Huh?" Joe said in surprise. "Dr. Michaels, stealing his own snakes? Why?"

Frank shrugged. "I haven't figured out why

anyone would want to steal the snakes. At least my theory answers a lot of questions about the locked door and how the fan was shut down."

He paused, then added, "That's assuming it was shut down. The crooks may have just lucked out. Maybe they came and went between cycles of the ventilation system."

"If Michaels is involved, how and why did he get injured?"

"Accidentally?" Frank suggested.

Joe sighed. "I guess it's possible, but it doesn't seem very likely."

"I'll admit, it's a stretch to believe it," Frank commented. "Still, I'd rather think of Dr. Michaels as a crook than Phil."

"One thing's certain," Joe said, pointing up the shaft. "The thieves got in up there and used the shaft to reach Michaels's office."

The moon was out, and some of its light filtered down the shaft. "We'd better get out of here," Frank said, "and figure out what to do next. As Callie and the others were looking for the switch to the fan they must have set off the alarm. I heard it as I was crawling along."

"Let's check out the roof while we have the chance," Joe said, touching the lump on his head gingerly. "I want to see what's up there."

After his brother reassured him he felt all right, Frank reluctantly agreed. "I guess it's okay, but we'd better hurry back to the others."

They quickly searched the area for something to use as a screwdriver. Joe found a thin steel bar, handed it to Frank, then followed his brother up the shaft. It was cramped at the top. Frank couldn't help but notice the fearful glance Joe threw at the fan as they inched past it.

The bar was clumsy, but heavy enough to do the trick. The grate came off, and a moment later they crawled onto the flat roof. A chilly October breeze whipped around them as they surveyed the view. Shadowy woods bracketed the building, and they could hear the calls and growls of the zoo's nocturnal animals in the distance. It was eerie. The atmosphere felt alien, as though they were standing on the surface of another planet.

Frank gestured toward the trees. "Anyone up here would be out of view from the ground," he said.

Joe nodded, then started walking across the roof. It was covered with fine gravel, and the penlight revealed footprints. Joe knelt to study them. "There were at least two people up here, maybe more."

As Frank panned the light about Joe pointed to the shaft they'd just climbed from. "See that?" He touched a spot where paint had been rubbed away to reveal gleaming metal. "Someone laid a rope to haul something up—the friction polished the metal."

Frank nodded. "Now we know how they got everything out." He frowned. "But I still don't get it. Who'd steal snakes? What could they do with them?"

"An eccentric collector?" Joe suggested.

Frank shrugged. "Maybe, but how many reptile enthusiasts are crazy enough to pull a stunt like this? I'm sure the police have already checked out any collectors who'd be interested in the snakes missing from the zoo." He grinned. "I mean, it would be sort of hard to hide the fact that you have a collection of cobras." He walked away. "Come on, let's check the rest of the roof."

They moved slowly, panning the tiny light. Suddenly Frank stopped as the beam illuminated some boxes near the edge of the roof. "Look at these."

"They're like the case the tiger snake came in!" Joe exclaimed. One of the boxes lay on its side, its lid lying broken beside it. Frank shone the light into it, revealing an empty interior. But Joe noticed something else in the flashing light —an unusual shadow making an S-shaped line in the loose gravel. A chill crawled up his spine. "Frank, look at this!"

It was another track, left not by a foot, but by a very large snake. As they drew closer to inspect the trail both wished they had a better flashlight. The penlight's beam was fading, and they could be walking right up on a very deadly reptile.

But the track led to the edge of the roof, to a drainpipe that carried rainwater down to the ground. Frank nodded in satisfaction. "I'll bet that's how Jake got away." He looked into the distance, then pointed to a small group of lights that shone dimly through the trees. "See those lights over there? That's the launderette where that little boy found the defanged cobra."

"Of course!" Joe exclaimed. "It crawled down the drainpipe and off through the woods."

In the feeble glow of the penlight, Frank and Joe made out some more impressions in the gravel.

"Something flat was here, and look here." Frank pointed to an angular gouge in the gravel. "It looks like the corner of a box made this," remarked Frank. "The thief must have knocked over a stack of cases in his hurry to escape."

"Yeah," agreed Joe. "The lid on Jake's box must have popped off—that's how he escaped."

A few feet from the broken lid lay a rope, which Frank and Joe guessed had been used to raise the cases from the shaft and lower them to the ground. Another box sat near the rope; it appeared to be intact.

"I wonder why they left this one behind," Joe mused as he reached out to turn the case and read the description plate on the front. As his fingers touched the edge Frank slapped Joe's arm away.

At that instant a hideous, angry hiss issued from inside.

The case wasn't empty—and its deadly occupant didn't sound happy!

7 Manhunt

Joe leapt away as though the case were a bomb. "Something's in there!" he whispered.

Frank aimed the light. The top was a fine plastic mesh that made it hard to see, but they could make out the form of a thick, brownish black reptile inside. The tag on the lid read: KRAIT.

"A krait!" Frank said excitedly. "That's a type of cobra. Why was it left behind?"

Joe shuddered. "Look closer—that lid's loose, and the thief didn't want to fool with it. I don't think this guy has been defanged."

Suddenly the snake stirred, and the lid rose slightly. A scaly nose poked out.

The Hardys searched desperately for something to slide the lid into place, but all they had was the short bar they'd used as a screwdriver. Frank handed the light to Joe and approached the case.

61

But now the krait was halfway out of the box. Worse yet, the penlight was flickering. Soon, they'd be sharing the roof with an ugly little killer with only moonlight to guide them.

"We have to do something," Joe said urgently.

Frank didn't answer. Instead, he shoved at the base of the case. The bar was only eight inches long, forcing him to get close. Suddenly the snake hissed menacingly, and Frank jerked back into Joe. The penlight flew from Joe's grasp and off the roof just as the moon disappeared behind some clouds. They were shrouded in darkness.

"I lost the light!" cried Joe. "What were you trying to do?"

"I faced the case out of the wind," Frank replied. "It's getting cold—maybe the krait will retreat back into its box to stay warm."

"He might," Joe muttered. "Or he might head for the nearest heat source—us!"

"Think cold," Frank advised. "We'll wait a few minutes, then check on what it's doing. We can't leave this guy here and risk its escaping."

The wait in the darkness seemed endless. The Hardys peered into the gloom, straining their ears for sounds of the reptile. When the moon came out, Frank said, "It's now or never!" They headed back toward the case. Suddenly Joe called out in alarm. He slammed into Frank, knocking him down.

Frank rolled across the rooftop, then raised himself up on one knee. Joe lay on his back, kicking. Frank saw something fly away. Something long and thin!

"Joe!" Frank's voice was hoarse. "Did—did it get you?"

Joe's laugh was shaky but welcome. "No. *This* is what got me." He held up the tangled coil of nylon rope the thieves had left behind, grinning at his brother's worried face. "Do you think our friend is snuggled up inside?"

Frank gulped loudly. "There's only one way to be sure." He stepped up to the case, reached out, and in one fluid motion slid the top in place.

A startled hiss came from inside, but Frank was already fastening the latches that secured the lid. The Hardys tied the case to the end of the rope and lowered it to the ground. Then they quickly slid down after it.

"This should be interesting," Frank said with a chuckle. "What will we say to zoo security when we return the snake?"

Joe shrugged. "It doesn't matter much anymore. The guards have already heard about our break-in from Chet and the girls, I'm sure."

They set off every alarm in the lab when they walked in—but only for a moment. The security guards were waiting for them. They marched the boys back to Michaels's office to join their friends. Chet and the girls sat glumly around the desk. All three were delighted to see the Hardys in one piece.

There was another familiar face in the room.

63

"I'm glad to see you're both safe," Con Riley said. "Now would you please explain what you've been up to? We've been searching that vent for you." He paused to look inside the case, then jumped back as the snake lunged up at the mesh lid. "And what," he gasped, pointing to the box, "are you doing with that?"

"Would you believe it followed us home?"

"Real funny, Joe," Con growled. "I wonder if you'll laugh when the zoo charges you with trespassing." He looked at the case. "Worse yet, you've been caught with stolen goods. I assume this snake's one of those missing from the zoo?"

"Sorry, Con," said Frank. "We were trying to help Phil." He quickly told Riley what they'd discovered on the roof.

"So the thief came down from the roof and left the same way," mused Riley.

"Looks like it," Frank answered. "But we think there were at least two thieves."

"Couldn't one guy have done it?" asked Chet.

"Well," Frank said doubtfully, "he'd have to be very athletic."

"Like Phil Cohen?" Con asked softly.

"Phil didn't have anything to do with this," Joe insisted.

"Maybe," Con said, "but the evidence says something else."

"What evidence?" Joe demanded. "You've got a tool anyone could have picked up, and

those snakes in his basement could be a plant."
Joe glared. "I think Phil's being framed."

Riley stared at Joe for a moment. "Would you say Phil needed money?"

"Well, he wants a new computer system," Joe said slowly. "It's not cheap, but it doesn't mean he had anything to do with stealing the snakes."

"I wish I could agree." Riley sighed. "But we discovered that ten thousand dollars went into Phil's bank account today."

Frank and Joe sat in stunned silence. "Wait a second!" Joe burst out. "When could that have happened? Phil was with us most of the time, and when he wasn't, you had him down in the station house. He didn't have time to go to the bank."

"Phil's bank is very up-to-date—they let you do your banking by computer." Con nodded grimly at the computer in the corner. "He could have given the orders from that machine while he wasn't with you—during the time when all sorts of interesting things seem to have happened."

The Hardys looked at each other in dismay. *Could* Phil have done it? He had imagination and daring and . . . Joe swallowed hard. "I don't buy it. No matter what the evidence says, I can't believe Phil's involved. There has to be another answer."

"Besides," Frank interjected, "who would pay ten thousand dollars for a bunch of snakes?"

Riley smiled. "All sorts of people. I had a long chat with Dr. Hagen today. She told me that snakes are valuable for a lot of reasons."

He flipped through the pages of his notebook. "King cobra venom sells for fifteen hundred dollars per ounce, Malaysian venom for about the same. Krait venom"—he paused to glance at the case sitting on the floor—"that's a mere twelve hundred dollars per ounce."

He slapped his notebook closed. "Tiger snake venom gets top dollar—more than twenty-five hundred dollars per ounce. And," he added, "a snake can produce an ounce a week. That works out to one hundred and thirty thousand dollars a year for the tiger snake alone. Add in the other snakes and you'd get about half a million dollars a year. Is that valuable enough for you?

"What's more," he went on, "the snakes are worth a fortune to places like reptile farms and laboratories."

Frank was stunned. "I had no idea venom was worth so much."

"What do they do with it?" Joe asked.

"Research, mostly," Riley answered. "Heart studies, things like that. Dr. Hagen said cobra venom has been used as a replacement for morphine. It's seldom used, because it's hard to get." He glanced at the krait again. "Not many people want to make a living taking venom from cobras."

"No kidding," Frank said dryly.

66

"Now you see why we want to talk to Phil," Con said softly. "The evidence is piling up, and he's not helping himself by hiding out."

"We've known Phil a long time," said Callie. "I can't believe he'd do something this dumb."

"Callie's right," Chet said. "There has to be another explanation. Phil has never stolen anything in his life."

"There's a first time for everything," Con replied. "For what it's worth, I hope you're right. But," he added, "from the evidence at hand, I'm afraid you're not."

"Security called to tell me there was another burglary. I got here as soon as I could." Grant Fizer glanced around the room at Chet, Iola, and Callie. "Oh, I see you got them." Then he saw Frank and Joe. "What are you two doing here?"

Without waiting for a reply, Fizer glared at Con Riley. "What's the word on Cohen?"

Riley shook his head.

"Well, when you catch him," Fizer said, "you can pass on this message: Thanks to his inept handling of my snakes, I have one king cobra, worth thousands of dollars, that may not live until morning." Then, in a softer tone, he asked, "Has there been any news of Dr. Michaels?"

"He's not doing very well," Con Riley began. A hiss from inside the krait's case stopped him.

Fizer's attention immediately turned to the case. His jaw dropped. "The krait!"

"You can thank the Hardys for its return, Mr. Fizer," said Riley. "They found it on the roof."

"On the roof! What was it doing up there?" He looked puzzled, then asked, "And what were *they* doing up there?"

"Trying to clear their friend," Riley answered for the boys. "They found some clues—"

"I don't care what they found!" Fizer snapped. "I pay taxes—taxes that fund your paycheck. I expect the *police* to solve crimes, not a couple of kids!" Fizer took a deep breath and let it out slowly. "Look, I'm very tired, and I'll have enough work for three people tomorrow. Why don't you just go away? I'll take care of the krait, then go home, too."

Con Riley reddened and asked, "Will the zoo want to press charges for trespassing?"

Fizer waved his hand, picked up the krait case, and disappeared through the doorway.

Riley sighed as he turned to the Hardys and their friends. "Well, I guess you can go. But make sure you don't pull any more stunts like this. Next time things may not end this well!"

On the way out Frank reached into his shirt pocket and pulled out the lab pass. "We forgot to turn these things in this morning," he told the security guard standing near the exit. "I guess we'd better give them back now."

Joe pulled his from his pocket, then paused with a puzzled look on his face. "Hey, wait a minute. The alarm went off when we came back to the lab from the roof. Why?"

The security man chuckled. "Your passes are useless now. Because of the break-in we had to reprogram the security system and issue new passes to the employees. We had to shut down to do it, finishing up about an hour ago." He nodded at the cards. "Keep them as souvenirs, if you like."

Frank and Joe pocketed the passes, then followed Con Riley to the parking lot.

Outside Frank turned to Riley. "You started telling Fizer about Dr. Michaels. How is he?"

"He's not doing very well," Con said soberly.

"Didn't the antivenin work?" Frank asked.

Riley shook his head. "It hasn't arrived."

"What?" Frank gasped. "Why? What happened?"

"Blame the paperwork," Riley said. "Exotic venoms and serums need special clearances to travel across state borders. Dr. Hagen said they may have the antivenin here by ten-thirty tonight."

"That's more than twenty-four hours after she requested it!" Joe exclaimed.

"This paper-pushing could kill a man," Riley agreed bitterly.

They said good night to Con and climbed aboard the van. At Joe's suggestion, and with Chet's hearty approval, they decided to stop for a snack before going home. As they munched burgers at one of their favorite spots, Chet, Iola, and Callie described what had happened while the Hardys were in the vent.

"When we found the thermostat switch for the fan," Callie said, "the alarms were going like crazy. Guards came piling into the office—"

"About thirty of them!" Chet interrupted.

"More like three, Chet." Iola frowned at her brother. "He told the guards we were at the zoo because we were working on a scientific paper about how animals sleep at night."

Joe grinned. "Did they believe him?"

"Would *you* believe him?" Callie giggled.

"Anyway," Chet continued, "they held us there, and one of them called the police, and a few minutes later Con Riley showed up. Whew!" Chet exclaimed. "Was he mad!"

Joe munched a french fry thoughtfully. "Is there any way that fan could have been turned on deliberately? Where was the switch?"

After Callie described where she'd found it, Frank said, "I guess it just came on automatically, unless someone operated it from the main breaker box." He sighed. "It's beginning to look more and more like Dr. Michaels was in on this heist." He described his theory to his friends.

Callie nodded. "It also looks as though he wasn't alone in his office when the theft went down. But all the clues seem to point to Phil and Dr. Michaels."

As the waitress brought over a piece of pie for Chet a familiar voice said, "Well, well, if it isn't some of Phil Cohen's buddies."

Joe looked up. "Mr. Bradshaw!"

"That's me." The reporter pulled up a chair and helped himself to one of Frank's fries. Frank glared but said nothing.

"What do you want?" Joe demanded. "Haven't your misleading stories done enough damage?"

"Just doing my job." Bradshaw shrugged. "A lot of folks aren't happy with your friend."

"Thanks to you!" Joe exploded. "Phil didn't do anything."

Frank turned to the newsman. "Why are you being so hard on Phil? That article of yours in today's paper barely contained a single fact."

Bradshaw grinned. "It's my responsibility to let people know when there's a threat to their safety, whether it's nuclear waste or a maniac who turns venomous snakes loose!"

Callie's eyes flashed. "I'll bet you got a dandy story out of the guy who was beaten up on Phil's lawn, too."

"You've keyed people up on purpose," Chet growled. "You're not interested in justice, you just want a headline—the more sensational, the better."

71

Bradshaw shrugged. "Is it my fault your friend is big news? I didn't ask those folks to show up at his place." He smiled coldly. "But it wasn't my job to tell them to go home, either."

"What exactly *do* you want, Bradshaw?" Frank asked angrily.

"The same thing every other reporter in Bayport wants," Bradshaw replied. "An interview with Cohen. You're his friends—I figured if anyone knew where he was, it'd be you." He looked around the table. "I've got people who would pay well for an exclusive story."

A stony silence answered the reporter, and he finally pushed his chair away and stood up. Bradshaw tossed a business card onto the table. "If you change your minds, you can reach me at that number any time." He turned and walked away.

Chet frowned down at his slice of pie. "All of a sudden, I've lost my appetite," he muttered.

A few minutes later, as the friends were starting their van, a sleek red sports car roared past the exit driveway, racing through traffic.

"That looked like the Pillari we saw parked at the zoo," Frank commented.

"It sure did," Joe said thoughtfully. "I wonder who owns it. If they lived around here, I bet I'd have noticed it before."

By the time they turned out into the traffic, the car was long gone.

A half hour later, Frank and Joe had dropped

off their friends and were pulling into their own driveway. As they did the van's headlights caught the gleam of another car.

"Hey!" Joe exclaimed. "That's the cops' unmarked car. What's it doing here?"

Frank killed the engine. "Maybe the chief's in talking to Dad. Or," he added tiredly, "maybe they have more questions for us about Phil."

Joe was just stepping from the van when he stopped, his eyes growing wide. "Speaking of Phil . . ." His voice trailed off.

A shadowy figure stepped from the bushes next to the garage. It was Phil Cohen.

8 Targeted for Death

The Hardys stared at their friend. Finally, Joe managed to speak. "Phil! Where have you been? Everybody and his brother's out looking for you."

Phil slowly limped toward them. "Man, am I glad to see you guys!" he said with feeling.

Frank rubbed his eyes. Phil looked totally exhausted, and there was a wild, haunted look in his eyes. "We've really been worried about you," Frank said. He glanced at the police car. "The police have an APB out on you."

"And a crowd gathered in front of your house today—people who think you turned the snakes loose on the town," Joe added.

"Yeah, I know," Phil said wearily, "and I had a hunch the police would be looking for me again."

"They think you're hiding out," Frank said. "Phil, what's going on? Where have you been?"

74

"I haven't been hiding out." Phil paused, looking sheepish. "Well, not exactly. After I ran off I wanted to be by myself. I took the bus to Ocean Beach and went for a long walk." He grinned ruefully. "I guess I didn't pay much attention to the time. By the time I was ready to come back the buses had stopped running, and I had to walk."

"That's a sixteen-mile hike!" Joe exclaimed.

"No lie!" Phil replied dryly. "It was real late when I got to my house, and there were still all these people milling around. I turned around, walked back downtown, and went to an all-night movie. Man!" he groaned, "have you ever walked that far in a new pair of shoes? I don't advise it. I have blisters all over my feet!"

The boys laughed but quickly grew serious again. "Phil," Frank said quietly, "the police found ten thousand dollars in your bank account and a couple of cobras in your basement."

Phil's eyes widened. "Cobras in my basement! Ten thousand bucks in my bank account!" His words came out choked and angry. "How? I don't—I didn't—" Phil's fists clenched in anger and frustration. "Someone seems determined to frame me."

Frank laid a hand on Phil's shoulder, but his friend jerked away. "Who's doing this?" he cried. "I suppose you two think I'm a crook, too!"

75

"Take it easy, Phil," Frank said soothingly. "We're your friends, remember?"

"Do you have any idea how the money or snakes could have gotten there?" Joe asked.

"No." Phil's face looked pale even in the darkness.

"Hey, we believe you," Frank said. "The money and the snakes must have been planted to make you look guilty."

Joe jerked a thumb toward the house. "Now what? The police are in the house, Frank."

Frank looked at the lit windows.

"Chief Collig's here," said Phil. "I saw him drive up." He sighed. "I'm sure he's trying to find me. I wish I knew what to do," he added miserably.

Frank said, "I don't think you have a choice, Phil. Let's go on in and see what's going on."

As the three boys walked into the living room Fenton Hardy called, "Hi, fellas. It's kind of chilly to be talking outside, isn't it?"

Chief Collig sat on the sofa, staring at Phil in silence.

Joe's jaw dropped. "Dad, do you mean to say you knew Phil was out there?"

Fenton Hardy grinned. "I saw your lights as you pulled in, then someone stepped out from the bushes by the garage. It was no big deduction to figure out who that was."

It was Phil's turn to be surprised. "If you knew I was out there, why didn't you come out

76

and arrest me?" he asked. "Frank and Joe said there's an APB out on me right now."

"I canceled it ten minutes ago," said Chief Collig. "Fenton convinced me to do it." He sighed heavily. "Phil, I have about six dozen unpleasant questions to ask you, starting with, 'Where have you been?' "

For a half hour, Collig fired question after question at Phil. Finally he said, "Phil, you don't have one good alibi in that whole story. The evidence tells me you're guilty, but my personal feeling is that you can't be that stupid. Fenton and his sons are convinced you're innocent. Con Riley has been arguing on your behalf since this thing started."

He stood up. "By rights I should lock you up, but Fenton says he'll accept responsibility for you." He glanced at the elder Hardy and said, "It's against my better judgment, but I guess I'll trust him in this." His voice hardened. "If I find out you *are* guilty, Phil, I'll throw the book at you. Good friends like the Hardys are hard to come by. If you're using them—"

"I'm not, Chief!" Phil interrupted. "I didn't do anything. I can't prove it yet, but I am innocent." He turned to Fenton Hardy. "Thanks for going to bat for me, Mr. Hardy," he said simply.

"That's what friends are for, Phil," answered Fenton.

Chief Collig turned to leave, but he paused

long enough to warn Frank and Joe. "You leave this to the pros. We can handle it. With poisonous snakes and venom thieves running around, things could get dangerous."

As Collig left Fenton Hardy said, "I imagine you fellows are bushed. You've had a hard day."

Frank nodded. "It has been a long one." A distant peal of thunder rumbled through the air. Frank glanced at the window. "Looks like we're going to get a little rain," he commented. "I'd better put the van in the garage." He glanced at Phil. "Considering the situation, maybe Phil should spend the night here."

Frank Hardy agreed. "Since I told Chief Collig I'd be responsible for you, Phil," he said, "that's not a bad idea."

"I don't want to put you out—"

"Nonsense," the elder Hardy said. "Besides, after that incident with the crowd at your place, it's safer to stay here."

"If you say so," Phil said doubtfully.

"Come on, Phil," Joe said, "it's no trouble. But," he warned with a grin, "you'll be stuck with the couch. There's a sleeping bag in the van you can use."

"You've talked me into it. Wait up, Frank, and I'll walk to the van with you and get the sleeping bag."

The three boys stepped into the night and strolled to the van. Lightning lit up the sky to the south, and rumbling thunder followed a few moments later. The storm was very close, but it hadn't yet started to rain. "Glad I remembered the van," Frank muttered. "I left the window down." Thunder punctuated his statement.

"The passenger door's locked," Joe said as they reached the van. "Want to give me the keys so I can unlock it and pull that sleeping bag out? It's easier to reach it from that side."

"Sure, Joe. Here they— Oh, great!" Frank exclaimed. "I dropped the keys."

"Frank," Phil called through the rising wind, "open the door and let the interior light come on. It'll make it easier to find the keys."

Thunder boomed again. "The light doesn't come on when you open the door," explained Frank. "We have to use the switch." Phil nodded, and both boys joined Joe in a search for the missing keys.

The thunder grew even louder as they bent down and searched the pavement for the keys.

"It's impossible to see in this darkness," Joe said.

Suddenly a blue-white lightning bolt split the sky—a spectacular electrical display that lit up the night. "There they are!" the boys exclaimed in unison, and they bent simultaneously to pick up Frank's keys. As they did they heard a strange sound—a dull *zuhtt!* Something flew through the van's open window and struck the driver's seat.

"What was that?" Phil asked.

"I don't know," Frank answered, alarmed. "It sounded like—"

Lightning ripped through the sky again. Before the thunderclap the boys distinctly heard the same hissing sound. This time something clattered into the side of the driver's door, inches from Phil's head.

"That was a dart!" Joe exclaimed. "Someone's shooting at us!"

9 A Terrible Surprise

"Down!" Frank yelled, diving beneath the van and scooping up the keys in the same motion. A third dart *thunked* against the van as he slid under the vehicle to come up on the passenger's side. In a moment he had the door unlocked. He ducked inside and slid over to the driver's seat.

"Watch it!" he called to Joe and Phil. "I'm going to start the engine and turn on the headlights." The van's finely tuned engine fired on the first crank, and Frank threw the transmission into reverse, turned on the lights, and backed the van around. The lights punched holes in the blanket of darkness, and Frank caught a quick glimpse of a figure ducking into some hedges.

"There he is!" Joe exclaimed, sprinting after the figure. "Come on! He's getting away!"

"Wait, Joe!" Frank called, but his brother was already disappearing into the foliage. Frank leapt from the van, and he and Phil charged after Joe and the mysterious attacker.

The chase ended at a dark side street. Even over the rumble of thunder Frank and Phil could hear the powerful growl of a high-performance engine.

They panted to a halt next to Joe and watched a shadowy car, its headlights off, flee into the darkness. Before it rolled out of sight, lightning flashed, illuminating the vehicle for a split second. "It's the red sports car!" Joe exclaimed.

There was no hope of catching the escaping automobile. Dejected, they trudged back to the van. Before they arrived, the storm broke and rain started to fall. Frank quickly slid into the driver's seat and rolled up the window. As he did he felt something sharp at his back.

Switching on the interior car light and twisting around, he inspected the seat. Stuck into the leather was a large, ominous-looking dart with a long, thin tube and a needlelike end.

"A tranquilizer dart!" Phil exclaimed as Frank showed his companions what he'd found. "I've seen them at the zoo. They use them to knock out large animals so they can work on them safely."

"I wonder what this one is loaded with," Joe said.

"Whatever it is," Phil said softly, "I'll bet we don't want any! I know it's late, but let's call Dr.

Hagen. She'll know what's in that dart, and I'd like to know how Dr. Michaels is doing, too. The antivenin must be here by now."

They checked in with Fenton Hardy, called the medical center, then drove off into the rain.

"Someone obviously wants to scare us," said Frank. "We're getting too close, and there's something"—he shook his head angrily—"something nagging at the back of my mind. If only I could figure out what it is."

The medical center loomed in front of them, and Frank parked the van. Dr. Hagen was waiting for them. "I'm afraid I'm losing him," she said quietly as the boys followed her to her office. Dark shadows ringed her eyes.

Phil looked alarmed. "Didn't the antivenin work?" he asked.

Dr. Hagen closed her eyes. "The antivenin still hasn't arrived."

"What?" Frank cried. "Why not?"

Dr. Hagen sighed. "Delays and paperwork." The phone rang. She took the receiver, listened for a few moments, then said, "You're sure? Good. Thanks." As she hung up a broad smile crossed her face. "Finally!" she burst out. "The antivenin is at the airport. An ambulance crew is already there, and it should be here in a few minutes."

She looked up at Frank. "You said something about a dart on the phone?" Frank handed her

83

the projectile. She turned it over in her hands, being careful not to prick herself. "Where did you get this?"

"Someone tried to shoot us with it," Joe said.

"We'd like to know what's in it," Frank added.

"Hmm," Dr. Hagen murmured, then she glanced at her watch. "It will take the ambulance a few minutes to get here with the serum. Let's step down to the lab, put this substance through the computer, and see what we come up with."

They followed her to the research lab, where she drained a few tiny drops from the dart into a small glass vial. The vial went into a cylinder attached to an enormous computer. "The computer analyzes the substance automatically," she said.

Joe looked confused. "If you can do that," he asked, "why can't you analyze Dr. Michaels's blood and see what he's been poisoned with?"

"It's not that simple, Joe," she said. "We have a pure sample to work with in your dart. Unfortunately, snake venom blends with blood very quickly, changing its composition. To make matters worse, Dr. Michaels's immunity treatments complicate the process, since he already had venom in his system. I tried to analyze his blood, but the readings came out garbled."

Suddenly a look of annoyance passed over her

face. "I forgot to call the duty nurse to notify her that the antivenin is on its way. She has to get Dr. Michaels prepped for treatment." She picked up the lab phone and dialed. Then she slammed the phone down. "The phone in Dr. Michaels's room is unplugged. We shut it off."

"Shut it off?" Phil exclaimed. "Why?"

"Some reporter has been calling every fifteen minutes asking to talk to Dr. Michaels. It was disturbing my staff, so we finally disconnected the phone. Now I'll have to run up there and tell the duty nurse in person. Reporters!" she snorted.

The boys looked at each other and muttered angrily, "Bradshaw!"

Dr. Hagen looked startled. "Yes, I believe that was the name he gave," she said. "I hate to leave before programming the computer, but the nurse must be notified."

"Can we help?" Joe asked.

"Yes," she replied. "Could you pop up to Dr. Michaels's room and tell the nurse on duty to expect the serum in about ten or fifteen minutes?"

"No problem," Joe said.

"I'll go with you," Frank said. Then he grinned ruefully. "In all the excitement, I left the keys in the van. It'd be a real climax to the day to have it stolen."

As the Hardys passed the front desk, where

85

one hallway led out of the building and another split off to the wards, they met an ambulance driver hurrying toward them.

"Is that the antivenin for Dr. Hagen?" Joe asked. The man nodded. "I'll notify the duty nurse, then," Joe said, turning down the hall and walking briskly toward the ICU unit where Dr. Michaels was fighting for his life.

The medic called after him, "This stuff was refrigerated. It'll take a few minutes to warm it to body temperature. Inject it like this, and the shock could kill the guy."

Joe nodded as he trotted away. Frank called after him, "I'll be back in a minute, Joe, just as soon as I get the keys."

The duty nurse listened attentively as Joe explained that the antivenin had arrived.

"Tell Dr. Hagen not to worry," she said. "I'll take care of everything. She's already left instructions for his treatment, and she needs to get some rest." She glanced at her watch. "As soon as the serum is warmed, I'll begin the treatment."

Joe thanked her and left, glancing down the hallway leading to the entrance. Frank had not yet returned.

As Joe pushed open the doors leading into the research lab he stopped in surprise. Dr. Hagen lay on the floor motionless, and Phil Cohen stood over her with his back to the door. The lab was a shambles, and Joe saw instantly that the dart that had been lying on a plate next to the computer was no longer there.

Suddenly Phil turned toward him. Blood was running down his forehead, and his face was a mask of pure animal fury. In his right hand he held a heavy steel lab bottle.

Before Joe could even say a word, Phil charged him, swinging the heavy bottle in a wide, deadly arc.

10 Needle of Death

"Phil!" Joe shouted, throwing an arm up to block the savage blow. Phil's wrist slammed into Joe's arm with shattering impact. The steel bottle flew from Phil's grasp, clattering to the floor.

"Phil, what's wrong with you?" cried Joe.

His friend backed away slowly and wiped an arm across his face. It came away bloody. "Joe?" he asked, blinking. "Is that you?"

"Phil, what have you done?" he demanded.

"What have I . . ." Phil began, staring at the blood on his hand. There was a nasty gash on his forehead.

Joe walked cautiously around Phil to a paper towel dispenser and pulled a few sheets out. "Here, use these," he commanded. Then, keeping Phil in front of him, he turned his attention to Dr. Hagen.

Phil daubed his cut with the towels, then

walked to a sink and ran the water. As Joe knelt next to Dr. Hagen and felt her wrist for a pulse Phil appeared back at his side. He gazed down at Dr. Hagen's inert body and suddenly seemed to realize what the scene must look like.

"Joe, I didn't . . ." He glanced at the heavy metal bottle lying on the floor and shuddered. "Joe, honest, it's not like you're thinking."

"You can tell me later, Phil," Joe said quietly. "Right now I've got to make sure Dr. Hagen is all right."

Joe shook the doctor gently. "Dr. Hagen. Do you hear me?"

She groaned, and her eyelids fluttered. "What? What happened?" She struggled to sit up. "Oh, my head," she moaned. Joe reached out and led her to a chair.

"Can you tell me what happened, Phil?" asked Joe after he'd gotten the doctor a glass of water.

"I—I don't know. Dr. Hagen asked me to get some papers from her desk. When I stepped into the hall, someone hit me over the head."

Phil stared at Dr. Hagen's inert form uneasily. "When I came around, blood kept running in my eyes, and I couldn't see. I came back in here and found her lying there."

He touched the bottle. "This was lying next to her. I was just going to see if she was all right when I heard you at the door. What if it was the same guy who bashed me coming back to finish the job? I couldn't see, and—"

His voice broke for a moment, and he stopped and took a deep, choked breath, then rubbed his hands over his face. When he spoke, his words were muffled. "Joe, I don't know what happened!"

Just then, Frank burst in. "What's going on?"

"Someone conked Dr. Hagen and me over the head," Phil answered, then added sheepishly, "and then I tried to hit Joe with a steel bottle."

"Whoever it was got the dart, too," Joe added, pointing at the empty lab plate.

"They took the dart?" Dr. Hagen said. Some of the color had returned to her face, and a grim smile touched her lips. "If he was trying to hide whatever that dart was loaded with, he made a mistake," she said angrily. "It's been fed to the computer already. We'll have the results soon." As she spoke the machine beeped, and a printer started to chatter. When it stopped she tore off the printout and read the results. A puzzled frown creased her face. "Odd," she murmured, rubbing at the knot that had formed on the back of her head.

"What's odd?" Joe asked.

Her frown deepened. "According to this, the substance in that dart was a combination of cobra venom—king cobra venom, in fact—and a very potent tranquilizer."

"Cobra venom and a tranquilizer?" Phil repeated. "What kind of a mixture is that?"

"A potentially deadly one," she replied. "It would cause the victim's system to slow dangerously if injected with the stuff. It—"

"That's it!" Frank exclaimed, and everyone stared at him blankly. "*That's* what's been nagging at me." He hastily explained, "While I was out in the van I looked at the hole the dart made in the seat of the van. The puncture looked just like a snake's bite would look, if that snake had just one fang. Don't you see?" He went on excitedly, "Dr. Michaels was never bitten by a snake! He was shot from above—from the vent over his desk—with a dart gun."

"Of course," Joe breathed. "That explains the single puncture mark and—"

"And his symptoms," Dr. Hagen interrupted. A look of horror masked her face. "Oh no!" she exclaimed.

"What?" Phil demanded.

She staggered toward the door, mumbling, "We have to stop them!"

"Who? Stop who?" Frank asked urgently.

The doctor slumped against the wall, gasping. "The nurse! Dr. Michaels!" she said. "Stop the injection of antivenin." She took a long, shuddering breath, then said shakily, "It's a tiger snake antivenin. It will kill him instantly!"

"Joe, call the police and get Dr. Hagen some help," Frank cried, then he sprinted down the

91

hall. He heard Phil trying to keep up, but soon his friend moaned and fell behind.

Frank raced on alone, ignoring the confused glances of the hospital staff. Panting, he burst through the door of the ICU and stumbled to a halt in Dr. Michaels's dim room just as a medic wearing a white smock and surgical mask was about to inject something into the scientist's limp arm.

"Hold it!" Frank shouted. The medic whirled, and Frank suddenly realized the figure was a man, not the duty nurse at all. "Who are you?" Frank demanded. A low sound came from the far end of the room. Out of the corner of his eye Frank saw the real duty nurse lying in a crumpled heap on the floor.

The man grabbed a tray from the side of Michaels's bed and threw it. Frank ducked, but the tray bounced off his shoulder with a numbing impact. Before he could recover, the man lunged forward, jabbing the hypodermic at him.

Frank dodged as the needle narrowly missed his neck. He knew with dead certainty that if the syringe landed, he wouldn't survive.

Frank shot out his foot, but it only glanced off the stranger's leg as he leapt back. The masked figure grabbed an IV stand from beside the bed. Frank dodged as the heavy stand flew past him. Then he jumped toward the man, aiming a karate chop at his neck.

His assailant was now between Frank and the

door. With lightning speed Frank grabbed the arm holding the syringe and smashed it against the door frame. There was a cry of pain, then the syringe clattered to the floor.

Frank tried to pin the man against the back of the door, but a knee shot up and connected viciously with the pit of Frank's stomach. Frank doubled over in pain, and the figure jerked free. He flung open the door, colliding with Phil and smashing him into the wall on his way out.

Phil staggered into Dr. Michaels's room.

"Frank! What happened? Are you all right?"

Frank was on his knees, his arms wrapped around his midsection as he tried to regain his breath. "Got to catch him!" he gasped. "That guy was trying to kill Dr. Michaels."

"Take it easy, Frank. I'll catch him," Phil said. "He and I have a big score to settle anyway!" In spite of his aching head, Phil dashed down the hall and out the exit.

Moments later Dr. Hagen, leaning on Joe's arm, shuffled up to Dr. Michaels's room. Three hospital guards walked behind them, followed by a doctor who was insisting that Dr. Hagen's injury needed attention. Dr. Hagen ignored his advice and asked him to check on the duty nurse while she rushed to check on Dr. Michaels. Frank staggered painfully to his feet and explained what had happened.

"You were just in time," Dr. Hagen said. "His condition is terrible, but if he'd been injected, he'd be dead." She smiled grimly. "I'll call the zoo. One of the techs out there can milk a cobra, and our lab can produce antivenin from it almost immediately. Now that I know what I'm dealing with, I can treat it."

She glanced at the pale figure lying in the bed. "He'll be okay," she said with conviction.

"So will the nurse," said the other doctor, helping the woman to her feet.

Phil returned, panting. "The guy posing as a doctor got away," he gasped, "but guess what he was driving."

"A red sports car," the Hardys answered together.

Phil shook his head, looking smug. "Nope, a staff car from the zoo."

"Things are finally coming together," Frank said. "We suspected all along that there were two thieves, and that at least one of them worked for the zoo. Where else but the zoo would you find a tranquilizer gun? And no one but a zoo employee would have access to a staff car."

He frowned. "Our trouble is, the thief could be almost anyone out there, from maintenance to security. But we do know something about him—he's got a bad habit of folding his trash."

"We know something else," Joe muttered. Everyone gazed at him expectantly. "This attack means Dr. Michaels can probably identify them."

94

Within an hour, Dr. Hagen was certain Dr. Michaels was on the road to recovery. "He'll pull through," she said wearily, pulling up a chair at the table around which the three boys sat in the cafeteria. "It might be a few days yet before he's conscious, but he's responding to treatment." She paused, then said, "You saved his life, you know."

"We're glad we made it in time," said Frank. "Have you heard from the police about the zoo vehicle Phil spotted?"

"The police checked with zoo security," answered Dr. Hagen. "As far as they know, no staff cars were used this evening. But," she sighed, "the zoo is nearby—anyone could have slipped in and out without being noticed."

Joe handed her a hot chocolate, and she sipped it gratefully. As she set it down, she commented, "I'll tell you something about your thief. He's an expert." The others stared at her quizzically. "Snakes are delicate creatures. If these people are stealing them for their venom, as the authorities suspect, they must know what they are doing. Nobody gets away with handling something like a tiger snake or a cobra unless he really knows his reptiles." She said softly, "You're dealing with skilled and very dangerous people."

She finished her hot chocolate and walked with the boys to the front entrance. As they crossed the parking lot she called after them, "Be careful."

On the way home, Joe asked for the third time, "You're sure you didn't recognize the guy in Dr. Michaels's room, Frank?"

"As I said, he was wearing a lab coat that disguised how he was built, and the surgical mask hid his face." He rubbed his stomach where the knee had hit him. "I can tell you one thing, though—he was strong."

"Athletic, huh?" Joe mused. "Athletic enough to hoist those snakes up an air shaft?"

Frank grinned, "I'd say so, Joe."

Phil said, "I don't know about you guys, but I'm bushed. I need a few hours sleep."

"Sleep?" Joe teased. "How can you sleep now? In just a few hours it'll be time to get up."

"Don't I know it?" Phil moaned. "But if you've ever tried sleeping in one of those all-night theaters, you'd really appreciate a nice lumpy couch."

The three friends were joking and laughing as they pulled to a stop in front of their garage.

Joe stepped out into a large puddle. "Well, it stopped raining, but I still got wet," he said.

Phil laughed as he came out. "Too bad you didn't whip out your magnifying glasses and check for footprints before the rain started coming down," he kidded. "Then we'd know the shoe size of the guy who shot those darts at us."

But Frank had stopped in the driver's side door, frowning thoughtfully. He squinted his eyes, sighting along the driveway. "You know, those hedges where he was standing are pretty big and overgrown," he said. "They just might have protected any prints from the rain."

Joe looked from his brother to Phil. "Well? What are we waiting for?"

He dug around in the back of the van and came out with a large flashlight in his hand.

All of them headed over to the hedges. Most of the area had been pounded by rain, and the light glittered on puddles of rainwater.

"Looks like a washout to me," Phil said.

But Frank pointed to another section, with several broken branches. "That must be where he ran through," he said. "It's a little more covered over there."

Joe pointed the light along the ground. "Bin-go!" he shouted.

11 Menace in the Meadowlands

In the glare of Joe's beam they saw a soiled bit of paper, neatly creased and folded.

It was ground into the damp earth by a footprint—a footprint that made Joe blink.

"I've never seen anything like that," he said.

The footprint *was* odd—absolutely smooth, with neither tread nor heel. "What do you make of that?" Joe asked.

"Would the guy come out in his slippers to shoot at us?" Frank said, obviously just as mystified as his brother.

Phil knelt down to look at the print, frowning. "It's a clean-room sole," he said in surprise.

"Clean-room sole? What's that?" Joe asked.

"A clean room is a section of a laboratory where experiments are conducted under absolutely sterile conditions," Phil explained.

He pointed at the print on the ground.

"There's a shoe designed to be worn in that kind of room. It has no tread or heel—that helps prevent dust from clinging to the soles. A scientist usually wears an elastic bootie over it to insure he doesn't track in a foreign substance."

Joe grinned. "Looks like this guy tracked a clue behind him," he said.

"I just want to make sure this is the right guy." Frank took the light from Joe and followed the tracks through the wet loam. Most of them had been obliterated by the heavy rain, but enough remained to lead him through the hedge and back toward the street where they'd seen the sports car earlier.

"It *is* the guy we want," Frank said, coming back. Joe had reached delicately into the first footprint. He picked up the paper, trying to examine it.

"Shine the light over here," Joe said. The paper was damp, and he unfolded it carefully. It was a receipt. Across the top, in block letters, was the name Hamadryad Labs. Under that, an address: 1432 Meadowlands Road, Jersey City, New Jersey. The receipt contained billings for a number of medical supplies, including snake venom!

"New Jersey?" Frank exclaimed. "Wait a minute! Remember that football ticket we found at Michaels's office? The Titans play in the Meadowlands Stadium."

Joe stood up. "So we've got a ticket for a New Jersey football game and a receipt from a medical supply lab in New Jersey."

Phil nodded. "A medical supply laboratory is the sort of place where we might find a clean-room environment."

"It certainly sounds as if we might find some answers up in the Meadowlands," Frank said. He glanced at his watch. "It's after midnight. Guys, I vote we hit the sack and then take off for the Meadowlands early tomorrow morning."

Phil's face was grim as he agreed. "With luck, we may catch up with the guy who's trying to frame me," he said. "I have a great desire to have a serious discussion with him—or at least fifteen minutes alone with him."

Joe grinned. "Yeah, I definitely want to meet this guy, too! But first we have some work to do."

He went into the garage and came out with a cup of white powder. "Get into the kitchen and get some water, Frank. We've got to mix this up."

Phil looked confused for a moment, then said, "Plaster!"

Joe nodded. "We're going to make a plaster cast of this footprint. We may not have a dart left, but we will have something to help hang this guy."

They mixed up the plaster, then poured it

into the footprint. "This will take some time to dry," Joe said. "Let's get some sleep, guys. We have a long ride tomorrow."

Before going to bed Frank made a quick call to the medical center and spoke to one of the lab technicians. According to him, Dr. Michaels had now received the proper antivenin. Though he was still unconscious, he was recovering while round-the-clock security guarded him.

Dr. Hagen had gone home after a physician had checked her head injury. Frank also learned that the syringe held by the man posing as a doctor had contained tiger snake venom.

Frank hung up and walked upstairs. That last piece of news hadn't been too surprising. After all, the bad guys had the tiger snake. But it did add something—they must have the expertise to milk its venom.

About halfway up, however, he stopped, struck with a new realization: Whoever was behind this was no longer trying to scare them off. They were trying to kill them!

Then Frank yawned—he couldn't help it. In spite of his realization, Frank slept just as soundly as the other boys.

On a nice day, it would be a two-hour drive to Jersey City. But the morning had dawned just as stormy as the night before. Frank's watch read 10 A.M. by the time he, Joe, and Phil reached the sign welcoming them to the New Jersey Turnpike. They could barely see the sign in the dense fog that clung to the ground.

After they stopped for breakfast at one of the diners along the highway, Frank pointed to a large six-wheeler truck that had pulled through the rain into the parking lot. On its side was printed: Hamadryad Labs, Jersey City, New Jersey. They were getting closer.

Soon after they had returned to the thruway, orange warning signs began to appear, alerting them to road construction ahead.

"What do you have in mind, Frank?" Phil asked as they drove cautiously through the fog. "Do we just waltz in there and say, 'Okay, who stole the snakes, attempted a murder, and framed that guy over there?'"

Frank grinned. "I like your style, Phil, but I suspect the bad guys may not be that cooperative."

His smile faded. "Hamadryad Labs may be a legitimate company. According to what Dr. Hagen told me on the phone this morning, the University Medical Center is one of Hamadryad Labs' customers—they buy special medical products from these guys."

He shook his head slightly. "I think we're going to have to play this by ear. Once we get to their offices and look around, we'll know the best way to deal with it."

"You know, I was just thinking—" Joe started

102

to say, but he stopped short as something struck the van with tremendous force.

"Watch it, Frank!" Joe yelled.

Like a huge white monster, a truck had suddenly materialized out of the fog. It lurched across the lane, smashing solidly into the driver's side of the van.

Frank fought frantically to keep control as the van ripped through a series of orange road markers warning that their lane was about to end.

He had almost gotten the van straightened out and back to safety when the truck hit them again.

"Hamadryad Labs." Joe grimly read the letters on the side as the big rig scraped past, thundering down the road.

Frank didn't have time to read. Tires howling, the van was now deep into a wild skid.

"Hang on!" Frank called, fighting the wheel. The wet highway felt like a skating rink as the van turned broadside.

To their horror, the boys saw the reason for the road signs. Two lanes had been removed from an overpass during construction. Where there had been a bridge was now a gaping sixty-foot chasm. Far below lay a busy thoroughfare, jammed with traffic.

The van was sliding helplessly toward the jagged edge of the overpass. In moments, they would plunge to their deaths!

103

12 The Secret of the Lab

Frank knew he had mere seconds to pull the van out of its fatal slide. The brakes were useless. There was only one way—a risky racing technique—but he had to try.

"Hang on!" he yelled, stomping the gas pedal to the floor. The engine screamed as the tires fought for traction. Suddenly they caught on a dry spot of concrete, and the van teetered on two wheels. Joe looked out his window. The van was balanced on the lip of the concrete cliff. The cars below looked like toys through the haze.

Still accelerating, the van shot forward with a scream of tortured rubber, darting across the lanes, through the barrier fence, and into the lanes of traffic on the other side of the thruway.

Horns blared and headlights flashed in the fog, but somehow the van came to rest on the far shoulder of the highway, facing the wrong way.

A patrol car soon arrived. "Are you guys

104

nuts?" the first officer demanded, striding angrily up to the van.

Frank stepped out on rubbery legs. Even through the fog he could see the heavy traffic on the highway below. Just a few more inches . . .

"Hey, I'm talking to you, kid!" the patrolman said sharply.

The officer's name tag read Trake, and his partner was Lyon. As Frank explained to Officer Trake what had happened, Lyon inspected the van. Trake frowned as he jotted information down in his notebook. "You mean someone ran you off the road intentionally?"

Frank nodded. "I'm sure of it," he said.

"I don't suppose you got a license number."

"No," Joe said, "but that truck belonged to Hamadryad Labs in Jersey City. The name was painted on the side."

Lyon joined his partner. "The van has a lots of dents and some tire marks down the driver's side." He pointed back through the fog. "The tracks indicate they lost control and nearly skidded over the edge before they shot across onto this side of the road." He shook his head. "That was one fine bit of driving."

As the boys inspected the van for themselves Trake placed a radio call. He called over, "You guys going to need a tow?"

"No," Joe replied, "the van's dented and scraped, but it seems to be okay."

"Well, your story checks out. Our dispatcher

called Bayport, and they confirm the identities on your driver's licenses. We should slap half a dozen tickets on you"—he smiled at the anxious looks on the boys' faces—"but we figure you guys have had a bad enough day without adding insult to injury."

Officer Lyon rubbed his chin. "You're sure that truck was from Hamadryad Labs?"

"That's what the sign said," Joe said. "Why?"

Lyon looked thoughtful. "Our dispatcher called them. They say their trucks are all present and accounted for—it couldn't have been one of their rigs." He sighed. "You're positive about the sign? After all, in all the excitement, and with all the fog—"

"I know what I saw!" Joe said stubbornly.

The policeman shrugged. "We'll check it out and keep you posted, okay?" He motioned to Trake. "We'll hold traffic so you can cross back to your side of the road." He returned to the patrol car, and a few minutes later the battered van was cruising down the highway once again.

Phil looked uncomfortable. "I hope this doesn't get into the paper! That's all I'd need about now—more publicity."

"They won't report it to the papers, Phil." Joe chuckled. "It'll just be our little secret."

"Our little secret?" Frank repeated. "That's it! That's what's been bothering me!"

Joe and Phil stared at Frank as if he'd lost his mind. Keeping a careful eye on the road, Frank hastily explained, "We've been overlooking something. Something really obvious. We missed a very big clue right after all this began."

"A clue?" Joe repeated.

Frank smiled grimly as he said, "Remember how you teased us for weeks about Dr. Michaels's big secret, Phil?" Phil nodded. "The tiger snake's arrival *was* a secret—a very closely guarded secret. If that's the case, what was a reporter doing at the zoo during all the excitement? Security phoned the police—nothing went out over the radio—so how did Bradshaw know to show up?"

"That's right!" Phil exclaimed. "There's no way he could have known about the snakes unless—"

"Unless someone inside the zoo told him," finished Joe.

Frank shook his head again. "Not just told him, Joe, they'd have to be working with him."

"Maybe someone let it slip," Joe suggested.

"No way!" Frank said firmly. "There were at least two thieves. One inside the zoo, the other outside." He grinned at Joe. "You proved that in the shaftway. Someone inside had to make sure the fan was shut down. And," he added, "no one could steal something from Michaels's office and the venom area without one very important item. We proved that when we returned the krait."

"The pass!" Joe exclaimed.

Frank nodded. "Anyone moving from room to room in the lab would set off alarms without a pass." He pulled the bronze plastic card from his pocket. "This is a major clue," he said grimly.

Joe said, "Hey, we had another clue, too, but didn't see it." He glanced at Phil. "The screwdriver. Your tools were in the lab the whole time you worked there, right?" Phil nodded. "So assuming you didn't commit the theft"—Joe grinned sheepishly as Phil glared—"the only way your screwdriver could have been in that vent was for someone who worked there to plant it. We messed up, too," he continued excitedly, "because there's no way that screwdriver could have been left at that end of the vent accidentally!"

"Of course!" Frank exclaimed. "The grates were fastened. How could they have done it without using a screwdriver at both ends of the shaft? If they'd used Phil's, they would have had to take it with them. But they didn't. Phil's was a plant, *meant* to be found!"

Phil nodded slowly. "It all makes sense. I meant to tell you," he added. "I picked up a sort of clue this morning myself."

"You did?" Joe exclaimed. "How? You've been with us ever since last night."

"Found it in your dad's dictionary." Phil chuckled. "Do either of you know what hamadryad is?" Both Hardys shook their heads. "It's another name," Phil said quietly, "for the king cobra."

"Unless I'm wrong," Frank said grimly, "the Hamadryad Lab extracts, processes, and ships stolen venom. After all," he continued, "the places that buy venom are respectable outfits. Remember the hassle Dr. Hagen went through trying to get antivenin shipped in?"

He grinned ruefully. "That was another clue, if we'd only realized it. The thieves would need a legitimate means of selling the venom."

"This is our exit," Joe said. "According to the road map, turn left and we're there."

Frank exited the toll road and drove slowly past a huge expanse of chain-link fence. Beyond the fence, masked in fog, was a squat, sprawling structure with a number of vans and trucks backed up to loading bays. A sign above the main gate said: Hamadryad Laboratory and Medical Supply Company. Parked in a space in front of the office was a sleek red sports car.

"Frank, do you see it?" Joe asked.

"I see the car," his brother replied grimly. "I think it's time we talked to its owner!"

Frank pulled in at the far end of the property, parking about a foot away from the fence. "Ready to pay this place an unofficial visit?" he asked.

Phil chuckled. "I'm already under suspicion for theft. What's a little trespassing charge?"

They climbed to the roof of the van, then took

109

an easy hop over the fence. As they slipped through the fog toward the lab complex Joe glanced back. The van was only a hazy gray shadow.

"I sure hope it's as easy to get out of this place as it was to get in," he murmured, then he hurried to catch up with Frank and Phil.

When they reached the rear of the building they could hear the rumble of machinery inside. But none of the doors in the back was unlocked. Joe tentatively peeked around the corner of the building. "There's a line of trucks over here and a couple of empty loading bays at the other end. We might be able to get in there."

"Won't someone spot us?" Phil protested.

"Probably," Frank said, "but I'm hoping they'll think we belong here." He gestured at the building. "This is a big place. I doubt if everyone knows everyone else."

"Come on," said Joe. "Let's do it!" Without waiting for a reply he stepped around the corner of the building—and smack into a burly man wearing a dark jacket.

"Hey, watch it, kid!" he snarled. He eyed the three of them suspiciously. "What are you guys doing back here? And where are your security passes? You'll set off every alarm in the joint!"

Frank reached in his pocket and pulled out his zoo pass, desperately hoping that the man wouldn't ask to see Phil's. The police had taken his when he went downtown.

But to Frank's surprise, after Joe showed his pass, Phil pulled a card from his pocket and smiled sheepishly. The big man frowned. "Break time ain't for another twenty minutes. I've a good mind to turn the lot of you over to the boss and get you canned. Now get back to work!"

"Yes, sir!" Joe said meekly, and he hurried away toward the loading area with Frank and Phil following right behind. They had to go past the parking area to get to the open loading bay. As they did Frank cut away from the group and walked nonchalantly around the bright red sports car, then hurried to catch up with the others. A moment later they swung up onto the dock and inside the warehouse portion of the structure.

Aisles of crates surrounded them. The place was buzzing with activity as forklifts toted cases filled with medical supplies across the loading ramps and into waiting trucks. Frank and Phil followed Joe's lead and disappeared down a deserted aisle of crates to a secluded corner.

"Okay, Phil," said Frank when they were safely out of earshot. "I've seen you work magic with computers, but where did you get that pass? Don't tell me you have some gizmo hidden on you that prints those things out for you."

Phil grinned as he pulled a small plastic card from his pocket. "We live in a plastic age, gentlemen. Behold my security pass." He held

111

out a bronze plastic card—from the Bayport Library.

Joe looked around. "I hate to admit this, but we may have made a mistake. Con Riley said a tiger snake produces a couple ounces of venom every two weeks." He motioned at the forklift activity on the warehouse floor. "With all the stuff they're loading, they'd have to have an awful lot of snakes to get that much venom."

Frank pulled the receipt from his pocket and pointed to the logo beneath the name. It read: Your Complete Medical Supply Source. "Venom would just be part of their business. That stuff out there," he said, pointing, "is just regular hospital supplies. The venom's probably processed in one of the labs. Remember, the antivenin that came from California had to be refrigerated. Let's see if we can find the labs."

"This area is obviously just a warehouse," Phil said. "I wonder where the labs are. If it has a clean room, it sure can't be out here." He wiped a heavy layer of dust from a crate.

As they stepped out of the aisle Joe once again bumped right into the same man they'd encountered outside. "You again! Why don't you watch where you're going? And who are *you* guys?" he bellowed, jerking a thumb at Frank and Phil. "His shadows?" He shook his head, then said, "I've never seen you around here before. What department are you in?" he demanded suspiciously. "And what were you doing back there? I think we'd better go see the boss."

Frank stepped forward boldly. "We work for Mr. Bradshaw," he said loudly, "and I can't say I like your attitude. When Mr. Bradshaw hears you've been interfering with our work . . ."

The big man's eyes grew wide. "Hey, I didn't know, okay? I thought—well, never mind. I was just trying to do my job. I—"

"Never mind," Joe interrupted brusquely. "Do you happen to know where Mr. Bradshaw is right now? We have an inventory report to give him."

"Huh? Oh, sure," the man said apologetically. "I saw him take the elevator down to the labs just a few minutes ago. You'll find him there."

Joe looked embarrassed. "Look, I hate to admit it, but I'm kind of turned around. If you could point out the direction to the elevator . . ."

"Huh? Oh, sure. It's at the end of that aisle. You can't miss it," he said, pointing.

Phil glanced at his watch. "Say, if you're planning on going on break, you'd better hurry. It's almost time." As he spoke, an air horn blared, and all over the warehouse forklift engines and activity stopped.

The big man looked relieved. "Yeah, I guess it is. Thanks," he muttered, and he hurried away.

A cargo elevator's door yawned open below them.

"Come on!" Phil exclaimed. As they moved down the aisle the man had indicated, Phil looked at Frank strangely. "Where'd you come up with Bradshaw's name, Frank? How did you know he was in charge?"

"Remember that little side trip I took coming in, when I walked around that red Pillari?" The boys nodded. "The registration was in the glove compartment—with Bradshaw's name on it. So I figured it was worth the chance."

"I'm glad it paid off," Joe said. "I don't think I want to find out what happens to trespassers in this place!"

They halted in front of a big open-platform elevator, the kind used to raise freight.

"I think it's better if we're not spotted down there," Frank said. "We were able to bluff our way through in the warehouse, but I imagine security is a lot tighter in the labs." His companions nodded in agreement. "Let's see if there's a way to get down there without taking the elevator."

A few moments later Phil called out. When Frank and Joe joined him he pointed to a small trapdoor in the floor of the elevator platform with a ring set in one end. "It's an inspection shaft for the elevator."

Phil pulled the ring, and a small wooden door opened in the floor of the platform. In a moment all three boys had slipped into the dark hole, climbing down steel rungs set in the concrete walls of the elevator shaft. They'd just stepped to the floor of the well, searching for an exit, when a mechanical sound above brought their heads up.

The massive floor of the elevator began to descend, and they had nowhere to go.

In moments they would be crushed.

13 A Hero's Death?

"Frank, what'll we do?" Joe asked hoarsely.

"Down!" Frank commanded. "It's our only chance."

They dropped to the floor and hugged it, trying to flatten themselves as much as possible. The lift descended like a giant press. It was three feet above them . . . two feet . . . a foot. Six inches above their backs it shuddered to a stop. The boys could hear voices and footsteps above them, and in a few moments the sounds faded.

"Let's get out of here!" Phil said urgently. "We were lucky this time, but the platform may drop some more if they put a load on it!"

Frank and Phil followed Joe back to the access door. Joe pushed it up cautiously and looked around. "I don't see anyone," he whispered. "Maybe everyone is taking a break." They were soon free of the cramped space and found themselves facing a long, sterile-looking corridor. "Looks like we should find the lab around here."

"Let's go!" Phil urged. "I feel like a sitting duck out here in the open."

They crept silently to the end of the hallway and slipped through a door. Plate-glass windows were set waist-high in concrete-block walls. Through them the boys could see people in lab smocks moving back and forth, sipping coffee, laughing and talking. Joe had been right. The lab employees were on break, too.

"Come on," Frank whispered. "We need a place to hide before their break ends." They hurried down the corridor, crouching to stay beneath the windows.

Joe silently pointed to a familiar device. Slots set in the walls next to the doorframes took the place of doorknobs. The security system was set up exactly like the one at the zoo. They'd need a pass card to enter any of the rooms! Otherwise, they were trapped in the open corridor.

Frank said, "We have to find an unlocked room." He glanced at his watch. "Their break isn't going to last much longer. Come on!" He slipped down the hall. The passage ended, and another tunnel-like hallway branched to the right.

As they reached the corner they heard the whistle blow, followed by the sound of doors opening and people talking and moving about. They ducked around the corner as a lab door

117

behind them slid open. Footsteps echoed away from them.

"That was close!" Joe breathed.

"We can't slink around hallways forever," Frank muttered. "There's an open door down there. Let's check it out."

They inched toward the door, stopping to peer through the window in the wall before entering the room.

"Wow!" Phil exclaimed. "Look at this!"

The room's walls were lined with glass cages. A lab tech, his back to them, was working in front of one case. He turned slightly, and they could see he held a snake securely in his hands. Even through the heavy glass they could hear the angry buzzing from the rattles on its tail.

"A timber rattler," Phil whispered. "I saw some when I went hiking up north."

As they watched, the handler placed the rattlesnake in a case, secured the top, then went to another case and removed another large rattler.

"Diamondback," Phil muttered, "and a big one!"

The boys watched in fascination as the lab tech carried the long reptile to a nearby table, grasping the serpent firmly at the rear of its arrow-shaped head. As the snake's jaws opened the handler pressed the fangs down over a vial topped with a rubber membrane. A thin yellow liquid trickled down the sides of the glass.

118

"He's milking it!" Joe exclaimed.

Frank nodded. "Yeah, but it doesn't prove a thing. The zoo's not missing rattlesnakes, just cobra-related reptiles. We already know Hamadryad Labs sells snake venom."

The snake handler finished his task and returned the snake to its cage. Then, picking up the vial of venom, he opened an inside door and disappeared. "Come on," Frank whispered. "Let's check this out while he's gone."

The entrance was open. They moved fast, looking for clues among the lethal reptiles.

"Hey, look what I found," Phil whispered, holding a sheet of paper.

"What is it?" Frank asked.

"A requisition for supplies," Phil replied.

"Look how it's folded!" Joe exclaimed quietly.

Phil nodded, then held it so they could read it. "And look at who signed it," Phil said grimly. Grant Fizer's signature was scrawled across the bottom. "Why would Grant Fizer order supplies for Hamadryad? He works for the zoo."

Frank's eyes blazed. "I should have guessed. We've seen lots of paper folded just like this! Remember when Fizer handed Con Riley the list of missing snakes at Phil's place after they found the cobras? And the ticket to the football game?" Frank tapped the sheet meaningfully. "I'll bet he's—"

119

"Someone's coming!" Phil whispered urgently.

The boys fled back to the hallway and slid below the window just as the lab man returned. "We have to prove these are the people who stole the snakes or we're back to ground zero," Frank said. "I'm sure they're around here somewhere. The trouble is, I don't know where to look." He shook his head admiringly. "I'll say this. They have the perfect cover."

Suddenly they heard footsteps and voices approaching them. Frank motioned urgently for the others to start moving down the hall. They tried door after door with the same result: None was open. Finally, at the far end of the hall, Phil whispered, "This one isn't locked. Come on!" They ducked inside as footsteps sounded in the corridor they'd just left. A few minutes later they heard a door across the hall open and then shut.

"That was too close!" Joe muttered.

Frank motioned to a plastic guard that covered a slot in the door. "You have to use your card to get in or out of this place. I wonder why the slot's covered."

A heavy stainless-steel lab table was bolted to the floor in the middle of the room, and in one corner a long bench held a number of large bell jars, the kind used for experiments with substances in vacuum. There was no window to the hall, but a heavy glass pane covered one wall

120

on the far side of the room. A curtain covered the pane on the outside of the room.

Phil walked across the room. "Something about this place is familiar," he muttered, "but I can't figure what it is. I've seen this setup before—" Suddenly an alarm started blaring.

"Hey!" Joe yelled as the door flew shut. He pushed against it, but it wouldn't budge. "What's going on here?" he demanded. An answer came immediately as the curtain over the window parted and a face appeared—Tad Bradshaw's face!

"Well, well." He chuckled dryly, his voice coming from a speaker beneath the glass. "And they say reporters are snoopy! Apparently it's an affliction that plagues other people, too."

Frank glared at the reporter. "Bradshaw, you may as well give up. We know your game. You and a partner framed Phil and are using Hamadryad Labs as a front to sell stolen venom and antivenin."

"My, aren't we clever?" Bradshaw said snidely. "But I'll bet even the clever Hardy boys weren't able to figure out who my associate really is."

"Grant Fizer," retorted Frank.

The red-haired reporter looked startled, and his smile faded. He stared coldly as Frank went on. "It couldn't be anyone else. Someone from inside the zoo had to let you know when the tiger snake was arriving. And someone had to be

121

sure the ventilation fan was shut down when you climbed out with the snakes."

Frank gestured at the glass cases lining a wall behind Bradshaw. "Someone who knew how to handle and take care of delicate, exotic snakes had to be around to look after them. And I'll bet when the police check, they'll find Fizer has a nervous habit. I'll bet he folds his papers and even his trash into neat little packages."

For a second panic flashed in Bradshaw's eyes. "Very good, kid," he snapped, "but your deduction won't do you any good. I'm afraid all of you are going to meet with a tragic accident."

"Like the accident you tried to arrange at the hospital?" Phil said.

Bradshaw looked surprised. "You don't know everything after all. That was my associate. Fizer is a clumsy fool, almost as clumsy as the idiots working for me on the roof of the lab that morning. They dropped a stack of cages and allowed some reptiles to escape."

His eyes settled on Phil. "I'm surprised you made it this far without passes. We adapted the zoo's security system to make our little operation here snoop-proof.

"Oh, well," added Bradshaw. "You won't go any further. What a shame that no one from the lab arrived until after you activated the device that transforms the room into a clean room." Bradshaw's eyes gleamed. "Oh, I promise, I'll write up the tragic story properly."

"What're you talking about?" Joe demanded.

"Clean room! That's it!" Phil suddenly cried. "You can't get away with it! The cops will nail you for murder, for sure."

Bradshaw smiled. "Oh, I doubt that. After all, you have a criminal record. This time you met with an accident and took your accomplices down with you. If you'll excuse me, I have a story to write—a sad tale about three snake thieves." He laughed and slowly pulled the curtain closed.

"What's he talking about, Phil? What's going to happen?" Joe asked tensely.

Phil was looking wildly about the room. "This is a clean room," he said. "Some are sterilized by ultraviolet, others . . ." His voice trailed off as water began gushing from six-inch pipes along the walls. "Others," he finished bleakly, "are flooded."

"Flooded?" Frank muttered numbly as the water swirled about his ankles. "Flooded completely?"

Phil nodded. "Then pumped out." He looked around wildly. "Bradshaw's going to drown us."

The high-pressure torrent was filling the room fast. In five minutes the water was at their knees. In ten, the water lapped at the edge of the lab table in the center of the room.

"Frank, we have to do something!" Joe cried desperately, after uselessly banging at the door with his shoulders and fist.

123

Precious minutes passed as Frank continued to scan the lab, searching for something to help them escape. The water was almost to his neck when he suddenly shouted, "The bell jars! We have to get them."

Baffled, Phil and Joe swam after Frank to the submerged bench. Frank grabbed one and held it out for the others to see, motioning to the wide base of the container. "Use them like helmets. Turn the mouth down and trap a bubble of air inside." He slipped the huge bell-shaped glass over his head to demonstrate, then pulled it off. "Grab one and get to the table."

Moments later the three of them stood on the table, their heads bumping against the low ceiling, water lapping at their chests. Frank lofted the jar and said, "Trap air in it. We'll be able to breathe."

"For a while," Phil muttered grimly.

"Hey," cried Joe, "didn't Bradshaw say he used the security system from the zoo as a model for this place?"

Phil nodded. "Won't do any good. Your security passes are for the zoo."

"That's right," said Frank excitedly. "But Bradshaw may not have invested in new programming for his system!" He dug around in his pocket and pulled out the card. "Hold my jar," he called. Taking a deep breath, he dived down and swam to the entrance. The swirling water made it hard to see. Again and again he tried to

124

slip his card past the plastic guard plate over the narrow slot.

But the water pressure made it impossible to lift the plate long enough to slip the card in. Finally, his lungs screaming for air, he swam back to the table. Joe and Phil held his jar and its precious air supply between them. The water had reached their necks. Soon the only air left would be the tiny supply inside the jars.

"It didn't work," said Frank. "The pressure holds the slot closed." He held up his pass. It was bent and split. "I ruined it trying to stuff it in."

Very quickly, they were forced to poke their heads into the jars. In a few more breaths their oxygen would be exhausted and Tad Bradshaw's secret would be safe. Their bodies, thought Joe, would probably turn up on a beach somewhere, while Bradshaw would have an airtight alibi.

He reached in and pulled out his pass. From another pocket he withdrew his pocketknife with the broken blade. They had one last hope. Taking a deep breath, he dived. Frank and Joe grabbed frantically for his bell jar as he handed it back to them, but it flipped out of their hands, freeing a huge bubble. Joe had no air left!

Frank watched in agony as Joe swam to the lab door. He couldn't see what Joe was doing, but it was obvious from the way he was kicking, trying to gain leverage, that Joe couldn't use energy and oxygen at that rate for long.

At the door Joe inserted the stub of the blade under the plastic guard plate over the slot. His lungs ached and his head was beginning to throb as the stub finally caught the edge of the guard. He slid it off and inserted his card.

For a moment nothing happened, then there was a tremendous electrical flash. Joe was flung away from the door, then violently sucked toward it again as the door slid open and water gushed from the room.

Phil and Frank watched in horror as Joe's body floated slowly to the surface of the rushing water, carried toward the door by the raging current. His arms hung limply, and he showed no signs of life.

"Phil!" Frank screamed through the bell jar. "Joe's been electrocuted!"

14 All But One

Phil and Frank splashed frantically through the receding water to Joe Hardy's side. Joe lay face down, unmoving. Frank rolled him on his back and towed him to the lab table. Just before he started to administer CPR, Joe coughed and choked. His eyes opened, and he stared dazedly into Frank's face. "What happened?" he asked weakly.

"Never mind," Frank said. "Either your pass worked or it short-circuited the system. Either way, you saved our necks. Are you okay?"

"My mouth tastes like copper, but yeah, I'm —hey, where's Bradshaw?" Joe tried to sit up. "We have to—"

Frank shoved him back gently and said firmly, "Take it easy. Phil and I will handle this."

"We'd better handle it fast!" Phil shouted. "I think we've made some people very unhappy."

A door that led to the room Bradshaw had

been in had only opened halfway. As Phil and Frank stepped up to the doorway the scene that met them was incredible. Tables and trays were scattered about. Water flowed ankle-high across the floor as more water jetted from the ceiling sprinkler system that had been set off by the electrical short.

Worst of all, the rushing water had smashed a rack of glass cases, and angry snakes seemed to be everywhere. The lab people hadn't been prepared for the onslaught of water. Some were injured, others knocked down, and two were being held captive in one corner by a very large and irate snake. But as Frank and Phil stepped into the room four husky men were there to meet them.

"Get 'em!" the first man yelled.

Frank piled into the man like a tackle going for the sack. His shoulder caught the guy's midsection, and the air whooshed out of him like a tire with a blowout.

Meanwhile, Phil was battling it out with a short, wiry man, who aimed a vicious jab at his chin. Phil dodged, feinted with his left hand, and connected with a right to the man's nose. His opponent's eyes crossed, and he sank to his knees.

A heavyset, bearded technician leapt in front of Phil while another lab worker—tall and thin with spiked hair—wrapped an arm around Phil's throat from behind. The bearded man

128

stepped forward, intending to sink a fist into Phil's stomach.

Like a striking snake, Phil's right foot shot out in a kick that connected solidly with his attacker's solar plexus. At the same moment Phil dropped to the floor, as the arm around his neck let go. He turned to meet Joe's bloodshot gaze. The skinny guy with the spiked hairdo lay on the floor.

As more employees ran in from the warehouse they circled the three boys, who knew they were outnumbered.

Suddenly, a voice rose above the commotion. "What's going on here?"

A group of firefighters stepped through the door, followed closely by several police officers. "All right, everyone, freeze!" a cop commanded.

Soon everyone was lined up against the far wall. One tech, under the eye of a young officer, recovered the snake that was holding two lab employees hostage.

The Hardys and Phil took turns explaining to the sergeant in charge of the police what had happened in the lab. When they had finished, Joe asked, "Sergeant, what brought you guys here? I'm not complaining—your timing was perfect. I just don't understand why you showed up at all."

"When the security system short-circuited," explained the police officer, "both the fire and

129

police departments were automatically notified. It's a safety feature, in case of fire or burglary. When we arrived we found nothing wrong in the warehouse, so we headed for the basement lab, expecting to fight a fire."

"Instead," interrupted Frank, "you found us fighting for our lives!"

"You probably aren't aware," said the sergeant, "that Tad Bradshaw owns Hamadryad. He inherited it from an uncle and has lost money ever since. Bradshaw must have turned to stealing venom as a way to make some money."

"In the meantime," added Joe, "he hired a manager to work here while he continued to write. It would be the perfect cover—who'd question a reporter's presence at the scene of a crime?"

The police officer grinned. "Well, now we have our work cut out for us. We'll have to investigate which of these people were in cahoots with Bradshaw and Fizer and which ones are legitimate scientists."

He sighed. "Hamadryad's been around for years. They have a good reputation, and a lot of their work is legitimate." As they followed the police officer up some stairs that opened into the warehouse they found themselves staring at a confused line of employees who were waiting for transportation to the police station. Joe looked around. "Where's Bradshaw?"

"We don't know. He must have slipped out in all the confusion. We have an APB out on him, so it won't be long. He can't get away." An officer handed the sergeant a slip of paper. The sergeant frowned. "My men just did a quick inventory of the lab. According to the ID tags, two of the Bayport Zoo's snakes are down there, but two are missing—a king cobra and the tiger snake." He looked puzzled. "Now where could those snakes be?" he mused.

The boys wondered the same thing as they gave their statements to the police, and they were still wondering as they started up the van and headed back to Bayport.

Outside of town they stopped to grab a bite to eat. As he munched Joe commented, "The cops think Bradshaw and Fizer are running for it. In fact, I heard one say they've set up roadblocks and put out APBs in six states."

Frank shook his head. "They may be running, but I have a hunch they stopped in Bayport first."

"How come?" Phil asked.

"Money," Frank replied. "They'll need it to make a getaway, and I'll bet it's hidden there."

"Why not up in the Meadowlands?" Joe asked, surprised. "How did you come up with that theory?"

"From Phil," Frank said with a mysterious grin.

131

"Me!" Phil exclaimed. "How did I become a part of this deduction?"

"Because you have—or at least had—ten thousand dollars in the bank, until the police confiscated it," Frank replied, "and it was there almost immediately after all this began."

"Well, sure! They planted it in my account. We already knew that," Phil said.

"Think about it," Frank said. "They obviously intended to frame you from the start. All the clues point to it. Ten grand was peanuts to them. Their snake operation was worth millions. I think they kept a stash of money somewhere nearby so they could get it fast, just in case anything went wrong. They used some of it to incriminate you."

Joe sipped his shake thoughtfully. "That means they're still in Bayport, unless they've already gathered up their cash and run for it. If I were they, I'd have kept that money close. My guess is it's somewhere in the zoo."

"I'll bet you're right!" Phil said excitedly. "Let's get over there and see if we can find them."

Frank chuckled at his friend's eagerness as they paid their bill and walked to the van. "Those two may be long gone, Phil, but I'll call Chief Collig and tell him my theory anyway. It might make a difference in how they handle the investigation."

They stopped by Phil's so he could get some

clean clothes. The sun had set, and a cold, gusty wind was blowing from the north by the time they pulled in the Hardy driveway. Joe glanced up at the house. "Mom and Dad must be out. There are no lights on."

"They must have gone with someone, then," Frank commented, pointing to the family car parked in the drive. He grinned at Phil. "Hand me that sleeping bag back there, Phil. Last night, in all the excitement, we forgot to take it in with us."

Phil shrugged. "The couch and blanket were just fine, but I'll take this for tonight." He handed the sleeping bag to Frank, then picked up his gym bag filled with clean clothes and stepped out of the van.

The boys walked to the house and paused as Joe started to insert his key into the lock. "That's funny," Joe said, a puzzled frown clouding his face, "the door's unlocked."

Frank muttered, "That's not like Mom and Dad."

Joe pushed the door open. He thought he heard a muffled sound from the living room. Stopping in the entryway, he flipped on the living room lights, then stood transfixed with horror.

Fenton and Laura Hardy were seated on the couch, bound and gagged. Tad Bradshaw hovered in front of them. A large glass case sat between him and the Hardys' parents.

"Well, well, if it isn't the meddlers," said Bradshaw with an awful grin. "And just in time!" He flung the case open. "Say goodbye to your parents."

A mottled black- and orange-speckled snake slithered from the case.

"The tiger snake!" breathed Phil.

As the snake lay on the carpet in front of the couch, Laura Hardy gave an involuntary start. The snake became instantly alert. Its head raised, and a hideous hiss issued from the back of its throat.

Bradshaw inched slowly away from the reptile. "You boys have ruined my operation," he rasped. "Now watch while my little friend destroys your family."

They stared in horror. The snake was alert and angry. Any second, it would lash out and choose one of the Hardys' parents as its first victim!

15 Justice Is Done

Joe flung himself across the room at Bradshaw, who sidestepped the wild charge, clipping Joe on the head with an elbow.

But Joe's sudden motion had distracted the snake. "Phil! The sleeping bag," called Frank. Phil tossed it over, never taking his eyes from the huge snake rising to strike only inches from the foot of the couch. Frank ripped the bag open, pulling the zipper all the way down its side.

The snake now faced Joe and Bradshaw. The reporter had grabbed his snake hook to attack Joe. A vicious swipe narrowly missed Joe's head, smashing against the snake case.

The snake hissed angrily, confused by the noise and motion. It struck at Joe's leg, missing by a hairbreadth.

"Joe, watch it!" Phil cried as the nervous, angry snake prepared to strike again. Joe was barely out of the reptile's range.

Joe glanced over and paled, then tried to step away. Bradshaw laughed wildly. He swung the hook as if it were a baseball bat. It caught Joe on the left shoulder, sending him backward.

"Joe!" Frank shouted.

The tiger snake's mouth opened, and its head darted forward. Joe twisted desperately, but the snake's fangs struck his back pocket.

"Frank, it got him!" Phil yelled.

Phil's cry caught Bradshaw's attention as he raised the hook to swing a final time. That moment's loss of concentration was the only opening Joe Hardy needed. Even though his face was pale and a thin sheen of sweat was forming on his brow, Joe ducked under the snake hook and rose up, swinging his right fist from the floor in a devastating uppercut. It caught Bradshaw squarely on the chin, and he crumpled to the carpet like a paper doll.

But a movement from the couch, where Laura Hardy had sat in an agony of terror as she watched the hideous reptile's fangs sink into her son, brought the snake's attention back there.

It drew back to attack, but a green expanse of cloth settled over it. Horrifying hissing erupted from beneath the heavy sleeping bag.

"Quick, Phil, wrap it up!" Frank cried, lunging for a corner of the bag. The snake thrashed desperately, and Frank realized the bag wouldn't keep it for much longer.

"Watch it," Phil cried. "It can bite right

through the fabric." The spot where Frank's hand had been just a moment before suddenly jerked, and the boys saw the round, blunt outline of the snake's head as it struck savagely.

"Now what?" Phil panted. "Pretty quickly it's going to find its way out." He twisted the end of the bag to prevent it from crawling out between the folds. But the snake's scaly head poked out from the opposite side.

Without pausing to think, Frank pounced, grasping the serpent the way he'd seen the lab tech hold the rattlesnake earlier. The snake gave a tremendous hiss and thrashed about frantically.

Joe, on his knees in the corner of the room, had just finished tying Bradshaw with a length of his own rope. "Hang on, Frank!" he called.

Frank had no intention of letting go. The snake was now completely out of the sleeping bag, twisting its length in a terrific attempt to free itself from Frank's iron grasp. A coil wrapped about Frank's leg, and its sudden grip made Frank lose his balance.

He went down, his arms jerking forward to cushion his fall, and found himself staring down the open jaws of the deadliest animal on earth. Venom dripped from two-inch fangs, and the reptile's hissing was a continuous sound.

Laura Hardy's eyes were wide with terror. Her face strained as she tried to slip off the tight ropes that bound her wrists.

Fenton Hardy's face was beaded with sweat as he cried muffled words of encouragement through the gag over his mouth.

Joe saw the sweat on Frank's face and knew his palms had to be sweat-slicked, too. If his grip slipped just a little, he'd die. "Phil, we have to find a place to dump the snake," Joe cried.

Phil was already pulling the snake case over. He stared in dismay at the lid. "It's ruined. The top was torn when Bradshaw hit it with the snake hook. Now what?" he asked frantically.

Joe's eyes searched the room, looking for something—anything—he could use to hold the snake. His eyes fell on the bag Phil had brought with clean clothes. "Empty your gym bag!" Phil dumped the bag's contents and tossed it to Joe, who shouted, "Frank, put the snake in here."

Frank's eyes brightened, and he struggled to his feet. Joe held the bag open while Phil managed to get a grip on the snake's thrashing body. Soon they had the snake stretched out to its full length and helpless. But Frank was tiring. Sweat ran in rivulets down his face as he said through gritted teeth, "Hurry! My hands are slipping!"

Starting with the angrily lashing tail, Phil fed the snake's whiplike body into the heavy canvas bag. Soon he reached Frank's hands. All that remained was the head of the angry reptile. Joe zipped the bag nearly closed to hold most of the reptile inside, leaving only a gap wide enough for Frank's hands. "Joe, get ready," Frank said. "I'm going to stuff his head inside, then jerk my hands free. As soon as I do, zip it shut."

Joe nodded tensely as he watched his brother's hands disappear into the bag, still holding the snake's head in a death grip.

"Now!" Frank cried, his hands going up. Joe zipped the bag closed, then slumped to the floor.

"Joe!" Phil screamed. "Frank, we have to get him to the hospital!"

Frank nodded, breathing heavily. "I hope we're in time."

Joe opened his eyes and muttered, "What are you guys talking about?" He struggled to his feet. "Come on, let's set Mom and Dad loose."

Phil stared at Joe. "B-But I saw the snake bite you. You shouldn't even be able to stand at this point."

Joe grinned and silently reached behind him and pulled his billfold from his pocket. Two large fang marks had pierced the thick leather. "I think," he grinned, "I need a new wallet."

As everyone laughed Frank quickly freed his parents. Then they turned their attention to the canvas bag and its deadly contents. "I don't know about you, but I'd like to see that thing out of here," Fenton Hardy said.

"Me, too!" Frank said. "And I sure hope they don't want us to take it out of the bag."

As Laura Hardy called the police Fenton told the boys what had happened. "Bradshaw came to the door and told us they had captured the tiger snake. When I bent over to look into the case, he slugged me. The next thing I knew, I was bound and gagged on the sofa."

He put an arm around his wife as she returned from the phone and sat down beside him on the couch. "Then he overpowered your mother." He glared at the securely tied Bradshaw. "He told us he was going to pay you back for what you'd done," Fenton continued. "We didn't know what he was talking about until just now."

"I'm going to have nightmares about this for a long time," Laura said shakily. "If your hands had slipped, Frank . . . if your billfold hadn't been in your pocket, Joe . . ." She shuddered.

Phil placed a quick call to the zoo. As he hung up, a squad car rolled to a stop in front of the house. A few minutes later Tad Bradshaw was hauled away. When the police asked him where Fizer was hiding out, he just glared, refusing to say anything.

As the police left Phil said, "It won't be long until Fizer joins him. I just talked to Tom McGuire at the zoo. Fizer's been spotted skulking around the grounds. They have a full-scale search underway right now."

Frank glanced at the bag. "That means it may be a while before someone drops by to pick up our friend there." He sighed. "I'm beat, but I'd

140

like to see Mr. Tiger Snake out of our living room and back in the zoo where he belongs."

They were soon on their way to the zoo to return their deadly cargo. The zoo was expecting them, and the gate swung open as soon as the van pulled up. Tom McGuire came running up with pass cards, accompanied by two men who took charge of Phil's gym bag and its contents. Joe stared at the pass and murmured, "I'm glad I had my old one earlier. These can be lifesavers!"

Frank grinned at his brother as they clipped the cards into their shirt pockets.

As they approached the lab McGuire pulled his collar up to protect himself against the cold wind. "I spotted Fizer in the woods as I came on duty. I didn't know what was going on until Purdy briefed me. I told him where I'd seen the guy, and now the whole security team and half the police—"

His words were drowned out by the wail of alarms. "Someone must be in the lab!" he cried.

As they raced to the lab they noticed that the door had been forced open. Inside they could hear sounds of struggling, and then a dull thud. "Look!" said Joe, when they had reached the back of the building. "It's a policeman."

It was Rogers, the officer who'd inspected the vent. He lay crumpled on the floor, and a large, nasty-looking lump was swelling behind his ear. "He's out cold," Phil said.

141

"I have to call Purdy," McGuire said, and he dashed off to a phone.

"It must have been Fizer!" Joe said. "He has to be around here somewhere. Let's find him." The boys were joined by a large number of police and security people, but after a long search they still found no trace of the snake handler.

As they rested Frank leaned against a lab table. "This is weird!" he muttered. "All Fizer should be thinking about is escape. Unless—" Frank snapped his fingers. "The money! He's got to have cash, and I'll bet it's here."

"But where?" Phil demanded. "And there are so many security guards and police roaming the zoo, Fizer couldn't possibly escape without digging his way out."

Frank stared at Joe. "That's it!"

Phil looked from one Hardy to the other. "What are you babbling about?"

Frank slapped his friend on the shoulder. "Phil, you just solved the last of this mystery."

"I did? How?"

"Fizer went underground, literally." Joe described the underground network of heating ducts they'd discovered while in the ventilation shaft. "It's the logical place to stash the money."

"Those tunnels may even lead to other parts of the zoo where he can emerge unnoticed," Frank added. "Come on, we have to stop him!"

It didn't take them long to find the trapdoor leading to the tunnel system. The absence of dust around the seal proved the door had been used recently. The boys pried it up, and Joe found a set of flashlights near the security post in the lab. "Might need these," he commented, then he shone a light down the hole.

Just then a horrible scream echoed through the tunnel.

"What was that?" Joe demanded.

"It's Fizer, and he's in trouble! Come on!" Frank dropped down the hole, followed by Joe and Phil. The tunnel system was riddled with twists and turns, but Fizer's footprints were plain on the dusty floor. The boys' flashlights caught the occasional bright gleam of the metal fire extinguishers along the walls.

Another scream echoed down the corridor, much closer this time. "It's just ahead!" Joe sprinted forward, rounded a curve, and skidded to a stop.

"Fizer!" Phil shouted as he came up. "You won't get away!"

Frank grabbed Phil's shoulders. "He *can't* get away," Frank said quietly. "I think he fell over that network of pipes. Look at his leg."

It was true. Fizer's leg was twisted under him at an odd angle. Joe stared in amazement. "Look at all the money! It must have fallen from that bag. There must be thousands there."

The boys approached Fizer, whose eyes were closed. He'd obviously knocked himself out. As they watched, his eyelids fluttered and he opened his eyes. At first they thought the look of terror on his face was from the realization that he'd been caught. Then they heard the hiss!

"Phil, behind you!" Joe shouted. The hooded head of a king cobra rose up from the bundles of money. The boys backed into the corner.

The snake hissed again, inching toward them. Phil gulped. "How do we get out of this one?"

Footsteps echoed down the tunnel, and a moment later Chief Collig appeared around the corner. "Don't move!" he cried, then he scratched his head. "I might be able to shoot that snake, but if I miss . . ."

Fizer licked his lips. "Freeze it," he said.

Collig stared at the man. "Freeze it? How?" But Fizer had passed out again. Collig looked puzzled as he muttered, "Freeze it? How in . . ." Then his face brightened. "I'll be right back!"

So far, the cobra had been content to crawl about the stacks of bills, but something—a motion or vibration—caught its attention. It reared a third of its body into the air, its wide hood casting oddly shaped shadows on the tunnel walls.

Collig reappeared, lugging a heavy fire extinguisher. "Stand back," he ordered. "This thing is loaded with carbon dioxide under pressure."

144

He grinned. "When the pressure is released, it forms dry ice."

He nodded toward the snake. "Let's see if we can use it to cool down Mr. Snake over there." He adjusted the extinguisher nozzle. "It's going to get real foggy in a moment," he warned. "You won't be able to see that thing. So get ready."

Collig took a step toward the reptile. Its head snapped around to face him. The chief braced himself and aimed the extinguisher. A white fog spewed from the nozzle, and in moments the tunnel was filled with white, smokelike carbon dioxide.

"Can you see it?" he called. "I can't."

"Back up, Chief!" Joe said. "We can't see it either." But the officer stood his ground as the air grew thick with fog. Silence settled over the murky tunnel. Everyone stood still. Where was the snake? The gas wouldn't kill it, but the intense cold should have immobilized it. If not, it could be getting ready to strike.

As the fog began to clear Joe spied a long, dark form. "There it is! Right in front of you, Chief."

The snake lay stretched out, unmoving. "Well, it looks like I had a close call, boys," said Collig. The frozen snake's jaws were three inches short of Chief Collig's shoe tips.

Moments later, members of the zoo's staff arrived to take the snake—and Fizer—away.

As he walked with the boys toward the exit of

the tunnel Collig chuckled. "You know, I don't think I'm ever going to feel the same about fog again!"

His voice grew stern. "As for you guys . . ." He stopped, sighing. "What's the use? If there's a mystery, you're bound to be in the middle of it."

The Hardys looked at each other and laughed.

16 One More Snake

The aroma of barbecued meat smelled delicious. The Hardys' patio was crowded with guests. As Callie handed Phil a glass of iced tea he said to Laura Hardy, "Thanks for inviting me over. I was afraid I was going to have to cook for myself, and I've had enough trouble for one week."

"Why, Phil, it's the least we could do," answered Laura Hardy. "After all, you helped save my life from that snake."

"Which one? The tiger snake or Bradshaw?" asked Phil.

Iola laughed, then she glanced to where Chief Collig and Con Riley were seated, holding an animated conversation with Fenton Hardy and his sons. "Hey, you guys," she called. "Don't you know you're supposed to greet guests when they arrive?"

Joe looked up sheepishly as Dr. Hagen

wheeled Dr. Michaels through the patio gate. "Sorry," Joe said, then he introduced everyone.

"Not out chasing snakes, I see," Michaels said, grinning.

"I think," Phil said with a tentative smile, "we've had enough snake adventures for now."

"What a shame." Michaels looked crestfallen. "I'd been counting on you coming back to work for me. I'm going to need quite a few new cases built." He noticed Phil's sudden grin and then added, "But no more screwdrivers in the pocket, okay?"

Phil nodded as he shook Michaels's hand.

"Is there any more barbecue sauce?" Chief Collig asked, dabbing his chin with a napkin.

Iola handed him a squeeze bottle, then said, "I'm glad you and Officer Riley are here. I have a couple of questions I'd like to ask. For one thing," she began, "how did Fizer ever get the snakes out of the lab?"

"That one's easy," Frank answered as Collig struggled to swallow a mouthful of food. "Fizer was in Dr. Michaels's office when Bradshaw, who was in the vent at the time, shot Dr. Michaels with the tranquilizer dart."

He glanced at Dr. Michaels and Dr. Hagen. "By the way," he told them, "that's why a second attempt on your life was made at the hospital. When we took their dart to the medical center to be analyzed, Fizer knew Dr. Hagen

148

would figure out the venom combination, and he panicked."

Con Riley nodded. "You're lucky that the Hardys were around, doctor."

"Anyway," Chief Collig picked up the story, "after Dr. Michaels was shot, Fizer bolted the door from the inside, transferred the tiger snake from its shipping case to a portable snake case—"

"A tricky bit of work, that was," Dr. Michaels interjected.

"I can imagine!" Collig said with feeling. "Fizer passed the snake up to Bradshaw, and Bradshaw pulled the snake case into the vent. Then they crawled through the ducts to the venom storage area. There, Fizer dropped from the vent and handed the supply of venoms and antivenins up to Bradshaw. A couple of their henchmen hoisted everything onto the roof."

Con Riley continued, "By that time, all the security people were at Dr. Michaels's door, trying to force it open. Fizer just walked from the storage area to the back section of the lab, where the valuable snakes were kept, and handed the specimens he wanted up through the vent there. Somewhere in the rush he grabbed the wrong snake—poor old Jake, without fangs. Bradshaw closed up the vent, crawled to the roof, and discovered his helpers had dropped some of the snake cases."

Riley chuckled. "The scene on the roof must have been pandemonium, with all those snakes around. Anyway, you know the rest. They passed the remaining snakes to the ground and loaded them into a vehicle—except for the two cobras that Bradshaw took over to Phil's and planted in his basement."

"Oh, yeah," Con Riley added, "we did some checking. The breaker switch to the vent fan is in the breaker box in the same section where the valuable snakes are kept. Fizer killed the power to the fan from there and turned it on after he was sure his friends were safely on the roof."

"Dr. Michaels," said Frank, "maybe you can explain something to me."

"If I can," the herpetologist said.

"Why was the cobra in that tunnel with Fizer? Was Fizer trying to take it with him? We never found a snake case down there."

Dr. Michaels frowned. "You know, I had thought Fizer was smarter than that. He's an expert at handling reptiles. I'm surprised he didn't realize that the snake would flee to the tunnels."

Phil looked up from the hamburger he was eating. "Flee to the tunnels? What do you mean?"

"If you'll remember," replied Michaels, "the nights have become quite chilly." Everyone nodded, and Michaels straightened in his chair. "Snakes are cold-blooded creatures. If the temperature drops to near fifty-two degrees, they become dormant. Their systems cannot tolerate the cold for long.

"When this one was dropped on the roof, he sensed he needed shelter pretty quickly. I can just picture him slithering through the woods next to the laboratory, seeking a warm place. What he found was a vent leading to the underground heating system. Among the warm pipes and darkness, he felt quite at home. He staked out his territory, and when Fizer stumbled upon the reptile's turf, the cobra defended itself."

Callie, who was handing Dr. Michaels a soft drink, suddenly shrieked and pointed behind Michaels's chair. "Snake! There's a snake!"

Dr. Michaels whipped around in his chair. "Don't worry, young lady." He reached down and grasped a squirming body from the grass beneath his chair. "It's merely a harmless example of a Thamnophis, the common garter snake." He held up the black- and yellow-striped snake for everyone to see. "This snake bears almost no resemblance to the dreaded Elapid, or cobra, with which you've shared some adventures over the past few days.

"Great!" Joe said, reaching for the snake. "I want to show you how Frank grabbed the tiger

snake, and since this one is harmless—*Yow!*"
Joe howled, dropping the snake, which quickly
crawled away. "It bit me!" He held up a thumb
to Dr. Hagen.

Laughing, she looked from the wounded Hardy boy to the other. "Some people never learn!"

THE HARDY BOYS® SERIES
By Franklin W. Dixon

NIGHT OF THE WEREWOLF—#59	62480	$3.50	———
MYSTERY OF THE SAMURAI SWORD—#60	67302	$3.50	———
THE PENTAGON SPY—#61	67221	$3.50	———
THE APEMAN'S SECRET—#62	62479	$3.50	———
THE MUMMY CASE—#63	64289	$3.50	———
MYSTERY OF SMUGGLERS COVE—#64	66229	$3.50	———
THE STONE IDOL—#65	62626	$3.50	———
THE VANISHING THIEVES—#66	63890	$3.50	———
THE OUTLAW'S SILVER—#67	64285	$3.50	———
THE FOUR-HEADED DRAGON—#69	65797	$3.50	———
THE INFINITY CLUE—#70	62475	$3.50	———
TRACK OF THE ZOMBIE—#71	62623	$3.50	———
THE VOODOO PLOT—#72	62487	$3.50	———
THE BILLION DOLLAR RANSOM—#73	66228	$3.50	———
TIC-TAC-TERROR—#74	66858	$3.50	———
TRAPPED AT SEA—#75	64290	$3.50	———
GAME PLAN FOR DISASTER—#76	64288	$3.50	———
THE CRIMSON FLAME—#77	64286	$3.50	———
SKY SABOTAGE—#79	62625	$3.50	———
THE ROARING RIVER MYSTERY—#80	63823	$3.50	———
THE DEMON'S DEN—#81	62622	$3.50	———
THE BLACKWING PUZZLE—#82	62624	$3.50	———
THE SWAMP MONSTER—#83	49727	$3.50	———
REVENGE OF THE DESERT PHANTOM—#84	49729	$3.50	———
SKYFIRE PUZZLE—#85	67458	$3.50	———
THE MYSTERY OF THE SILVER STAR—#86	64374	$3.50	———
PROGRAM FOR DESTRUCTION—#87	64895	$3.50	———
TRICKY BUSINESS—#88	64973	$3.50	———
THE SKY BLUE FRAME—#89	64974	$3.50	———
DANGER ON THE DIAMOND—#90	63425	$3.50	———
SHIELD OF FEAR—#91	66308	$3.50	———
THE SHADOW KILLERS—#92	66309	$3.50	———
THE BILLION DOLLAR RANSOM—#93	66310	$3.50	———
BREAKDOWN IN AXEBLADE—#94	66311	$3.50	———
DANGER ON THE AIR—#95	66305	$3.50	———
THE HARDY BOYS® GHOST STORIES	50808	$3.50	———
NANCY DREW® AND THE HARDY BOYS® SUPER SLEUTHS	43375	$3.50	———
NANCY DREW® AND THE HARDY BOYS® SUPER SLEUTHS #2	50194	$3.50	———

NANCY DREW® and THE HARDY BOYS® are trademarks of Simon & Schuster, registered in the United States Patent and Trademark Office.

AND DON'T FORGET...NANCY DREW CASEFILES® NOW AVAILABLE IN PAPERBACK.